PETER O'SHAUGHNESSY is best known for his work in Australia, Ireland, Britain and Canada as a theatre director, actor and playwright. He is one of the leading directors in the world of the plays of Samuel Beckett.

He has also been distinguished for his many productions of the plays of Shakespeare and for his performances of such roles as Othello, Hamlet, Macbeth, King Lear and Shylock. For The British Council he has lectured on the plays of Shakespeare in many parts of the world.

In recent years three of his books have been published:

The Fabulous Journey of Mac Con Glin (1985):
A Rum Story: The Adventures of Joseph Holt — thirteen years in New South Wales, 1800–1812:
The Gardens of Hell (1988)

CON'S FABULOUS JOURNEY
TO THE LAND OF GOBEL O'GLUG

How Con came to the Feast
And, with the help of the Wizard Doctor,
Banished the Demon of Gluttony
From the belly of the King of Munster

Peter O'Shaughnessy

Con's fabulous journey to the land of gobel o'glug

Illustrated by Terry Myler

THE CHILDREN'S PRESS

FOR DANIEL

First published 1985 by
Sabrainne
This edition 1992 by
The Children's Press

© Text Peter O'Shaughnessy
© Illustrations The Children's Press

ISBN 0 947962 68 9

Typesetting by Computertype Limited
Printed by Colour Books Limited

contents

HIBERNIA

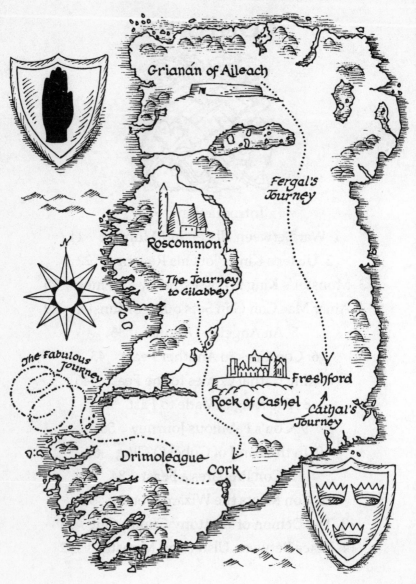

Grianán of Aileach

Fergal's Journey

Roscommon

The Journey to Gilabbey

The Fabulous Journey

Freshford

Rock of Cashel

Cathal's Journey

Drimoleague

Cork

introduction

he inspiration for *Con's Fabulous Journey to the Land of Gobel O'Glug* is an old Irish story, which may be more than a thousand years old, called *Aislinge meic Conglinne* (the Vision of Mac Conglinne). How grateful we must be to the scholar-monk who wrote down the story almost six hundred years ago, between AD 1408 and 1411, on a manuscript which now forms part of the Speckled Book (the *Leabhar Breac*).

Fragments of an earlier version of the story, probably dating from the eight or ninth century, may be seen in a seventeenth-century text in Trinity College, Dublin.

The *Leabhar Breac* also contains religious and other pieces derived from Latin, Irish literature and history, including the lives of Saint Patrick and Saint Brigid, the Litany of Our Lady, *Félire Óengusso, Céli Dé* and a history of Philip of Macedon and Alexander the Great.

All these manuscripts, now bound into a single book, were written by one scholar-monk, Murchadh Riabhach Ó Cuindlis, who worked at the MacEgan Law School (Duniry) at Cluain Lethan in Muscraige Tiré in northern Tipperary, now the site of Redwood Castle near the little town of Lorrha. It may be that all the manuscripts originated there, although some scholars think that parts may have been written down in the nearby monasteries at Clonmacnoise, Ely and Ormond.

Sometimes the Speckled Book is on display at the Royal Irish Academy, Dawson Street, Dublin, where it is held. Like all the books of ancient Ireland it is a beautiful work of art: The decoration of the capitals is simple and there are some fine interlaced letters coloured in red, vermilion, yellow and blue.

I acknowledge, gratefully, the advice and assistance of Dr Seán ÓCoileáin and of the poet Anthony Blinco. Above all, I am indebted to the work of two distinguished Celtic scholars of the nineteenth century: W. M. Hennessy, whose translation of *Aislinge meic Conglinne* was published by Fraser's Magazine in 1873; and Kuno Meyer, whose revision of that translation was published by The Irish Texts Society in 1892.

Writing of *Aislinge meic Conglinne* in The Irish Tradition Dr Robin Flower says: 'Mac Conglinne is an example of the type of truant scholar, the "scholars vagans" of European literature, the happy-go-lucky vagabond who goes singing and swaggering through the Middle Ages until he finds his highest expression in François Villon ... the tale is one long parody of the literary methods used by the clerical scholars.'

Such satirical elements are only dimly reflected in my version of the story, which is essentially for children. I have added to, and subtracted from, *Aislinge meic Conglinne* but the main lines of the original plot, which is part of the Irish heritage, are still there.

Peter Ó Shaughnessy
September 1992

1 war between ulster and munster

a long time ago, in the days when Ireland was a land of saints and scholars, it was also a land of warring tribes, and each tribe had a king of its own.

Once a year all the kings would lay down their arms and, for a week, peace would reign across Ireland as the kings and queens, with their attendant lords and ladies, came together at the Hill of Tara where they would pay tribute to the High King of Ireland, King Neill, and feast and make merry.

King Neill had been High King of Ireland for twelve years and he was growing old. Soon it might be necessary to elect a new High King. Some favoured King Cathal Mac Finguine of Munster, who ruled from the great Rock of Cashel, while others thought to vote for his rival and arch-enemy, King Fergal of Ulster, who held sway from the Grianán of Aileach, overlooking Lough Swilly and Lough Foyle. Cathal and Fergal had often done battle with one another.

'If I can persuade King Owen of Connaught to be on my side and vote for me, then for sure one day I will be the new High King of Ireland,' said Fergal to himself as his chariot wound down past Lough Erne and through the drumlins and lochs of Monaghan, bound for Tara.

11

Fergal glanced at his sister, Oonagh, seated beside him, her golden hair waving in the wind. Oonagh was beautiful, her cheeks as rosy as the apples that grow on the apple trees in the Golden Vale of Tipperary, and her teeth as white as the blossoms on those trees in Mary's month, the month of May. It was said that Oonagh was the most beautiful woman in Ireland.

'I will match Oonagh with Owen of Connaught,' thought Fergal. 'If I can arrange their marriage then Owen will be on my side when the time comes to elect a new High King.'

Before the first Great Feast (or Feís) was due to be held in the Great Banqueting Hall on Tara, King Fergal came to the High King and, going down on his knees, begged a boon of him, which King Neill readily granted.

Thus was it arranged that Fergal's sister, Oonagh, would

be given a place at table on Fergal's right-hand side while on her right-hand side would sit Owen, King of Connaught.

But Fergal's scheme was not to prove successful. For no sooner were all the company seated at table than Oonagh's eyes fell on a man who was sitting some distance away on the other side of the long oaken table. At once her heart leapt up and she felt the stirrings of love.

'Merciful God,' she thought to herself, 'what has happened to me. I feel quite giddy.'

Then a dread thought crossed her mind and, turning to her brother, she asked in a voice which she tried to make sound casual, 'It is good that all of you kings are at peace with one another today. Tell me — which of the many assembled here is your arch-enemy, King Cathal of Munster?'

'Well, he's not been given a seat of honour like ourselves,'

answered Fergal. 'There, that's him, at the end of table.'

Oonagh's heart sank. For the man to whom she felt ready to pledge her heart was none other than her brother's sworn enemy.

As the feast went on, and the goblets overflowed and the huge dishes and platters of venison, beef and game were laid bare, the merriment grew and the Great Hall echoed with high talk and laughter.

Fergal had already told Owen that he would be pleased (if the king so chose) to see his sister wedded to him, and so Owen attempted to engage her in conversation. But whenever he spoke to her she did not seem to be listening and never once replied to him. Owen thought to himself, 'Well she may be beautiful but I wonder if this poor girl from Ulster is in possession of her wits.'

Fergal, seated on his sister's other side, could not fail to notice that she had fallen silent. 'What's come over the girl today?' he thought as his teeth chomped down savagely on a leg of beef.

Oonagh had not dared to look again in the direction of Cathal but, when finally she did allow herself to steal a glance, her heart leapt up again — for Cathal was looking at *her*. And when their eyes met love kindled between them like a darting flame.

After the feast the tables were cleared, the musicians (the *ceoltóiri*) struck up, and the kings and the queens and the lords and ladies danced with one another. At first, Oonagh danced with Owen, who by now hardly bothered to speak to her. And once she trod on the big toe of his right foot, so that he went limping off the floor and sat down on a stool, muttering a curse.

And then the time came for her to dance with Cathal. He bowed and took her hand and they danced as in a dream but still not a word had passed between them.

As the music stopped, Cathal stooped down and

whispered to her, 'Saint Kierán's Well. Tomorrow morn when Saint Patrick's bell strikes eleven of the hour.'

Oonagh nodded her assent.

'That sister of yours,' said Owen to Fergal later, 'is a fine-looking filly, no doubt of that. But you didn't tell me the girl was dumb.'

'She's not dumb.'

'Tongue-tied then. Devil a word could I get out of her.' And he told Fergal that there was no prospect of his taking Oonagh as his bride.

Fergal was very angry. Before they parted that evening to go to their separate bed-chambers, he turned on his sister fiercely: 'Owen said you didn't open your mouth. Not once. He thought you were dumb.'

'I would never marry Owen, never. And he would not wish to marry me I'm sure,' said Oonagh in a defiant voice. Then, stamping her foot, she added, 'Anyway, I don't like the shape of his head. It's like a pumpkin.'

'If that's the way you behave you might be better off behind convent walls,' said her brother savagely, although not for a moment did he guess that Oonagh's heart was already given to his arch-enemy.

Every day during the following week Oonagh and Cathal would meet secretly by Saint Kierán's Well. There they would walk by the stream and watch the trout and salmon leaping over the little falls and making their way upstream. They wandered into the woods where they came across a herd of grazing deer. Rabbits scuttled across their path and back to their burrows, and squirrels gathered nuts and then scampered up the trunks of trees. And they loved to pick apples and munch them together.

And then came the day before the Feís was due to end and the thought crossed their minds that they might never see each other again. Hand in hand they walked by the stream and, for a long time, were silent.

'Oh, what a lovely juicy-looking apple,' said Oonagh looking up, and she plucked it from the overhanging branch. She took a bite and invited Cathal to do the same. Then, taking the apple in her hand, she cast it into the stream where the swift current soon bore it away.

'That apple will be a symbol of our undying love,' she whispered to her lover. 'It will twist and turn, it will overcome rocks and reeds and crags, and eventually, borne by the waters, it will make its way into the sacred river Boyne and along to its source, there where young Aonghus, the God of Love, has his shrine in a secret grotto.'

'I will write to you,' said Oonagh, when the time grew near for them to part.

'But your letters may be discovered.'

'Never fear, I will conceal them in baskets of gifts that I will send to you. And the gifts will be ... nuts and kernels and ...' Oonagh paused for a moment and then, with a little laugh, she said, 'And, of course ... *apples*.'

'And I will write to you', said Cathal. 'I have a carrier pigeon named Brak. He has carried many messages for me in the past. Even carried messages to your brother. He knows where your castle is. Brak is a rare pigeon. He is speckled. But, oh, how can we ever hope to be wed,' he continued, suddenly downcast. 'Your brother would never consent. He will never make peace with me.'

'Trust to the angel Mura.'

'Mura?'

'Mura is my guardian angel. And sometimes he shows himself to me, or comes to me in a dream. There are even times when he will disguise himself and walk among men.'

When all the kings and queens and lords and ladies were taking farewell of each other Cathal took Oonagh's hand

and kissed it; and, although he could not allow himself to be seen speaking with her, he lingered so long over the kiss that Fergal grew suspicious. Then he noticed that there were tears in his sister's eyes, as she whispered, 'Cathal, aroon.'

'Ha! Now I see why she would not marry Owen,' thought Fergal. 'I'll teach her to betray me.'

No sooner were brother and sister arrived back in Ulster than Fergal rounded on his sister and charged her with being in love with his enemy. At first she refused either to deny or admit the truth. Then, finally, exasperated beyond endurance, she burst out, 'Yes, yes, I do love him. There now! And one day we will be wed.'

'Pah! It's the convent for you, my girl.'

And so Oonagh was shut up behind the walls of a convent, which lay half a mile to the west of her brother's castle.

Weeks went by and then, one day, as she walked in the vegetable garden, she saw a pigeon flying overhead. At first it seemed to be heading for the castle but then it turned and dived down low over her head. Then it wheeled up towards the sky again and began to circle in the air, as though uncertain of its destination.

'How strange!' thought Oonagh. 'A speckled pigeon. I never saw one like that before ... Why, of course, it must be Brak.' And she called out, 'Brak! Brak! Here! Here!'

But the bird continued to circle.

'I'll try whistling to it. I know — I'll whistle that tune I heard on the tin whistle one day. It was called *The song of the birds as they come roosting back to their nests.*'

And, as she whistled, Brak came wheeling down and landed in the cabbage patch.

Hurrying forward, Oonagh lifted up the pigeon in her arms and, sure enough, there was a tiny scroll wrapped around Brak's left foot. And when Oonagh opened it out and read it her heart was full, for Cathal's love for her was warm and steadfast and assuring.

Lost in thought she stood there gazing at the high convent wall with the long tendrils of creeping vines that reached to the top. If only she could escape. But she knew that was impossible.

Her train of thought was broken as she heard the sound of chirruping high above her and there was Brak homeward bound. Soon he was a speck on the horizon.

'Too late. Too late,' she said aloud. 'I might have sent a reply. Oh Brak, why were you in such a hurry?'

For some days Oonagh pondered how she might send a letter to her lover. Then, one day, she saw old Paudy, the gardener, stooping down and picking beans in the vegetable garden and heaping them in a basket. From there he moved across to the apple orchard and began to pick apples and lay them in the basket. After that he went into the hazel wood and, when he returned, he carried another basket full of the very sweets and fruits and hazel nuts which she had promised to send Cathal.

'Do you think I might have one of those baskets? The one with the apples and nuts?' she asked the old man.

'But of course, dear lady. There's plenty more — an abundance. Take it and welcome,' said Paudy, handing the basket to her.

Then fortune came to Oonagh's aid. Or was it Mura? (For not a night went by without her praying to the angel.) She learnt that one of the sisters in the convent had a brother who was a Messenger named Michael, and this Messenger often carried letters and parcels down south, sometimes even as far as Munster. Michael told his sister that he would be only too ready to deliver baskets of fruit to King Cathal for, although he knew of the enmity between the two kings, 'What harm could there be in a gift like that?' he thought.

And so the lovers began to communicate with each other.

Meanwhile Fergal's hatred for Cathal grew more intense day by day. 'But for him and that obstinate sister of mine I might have been set to be High King of Ireland,' he thought. 'The old king can't live that much longer, for I am told he is ailing.'

Another bitter pill that Fergal was obliged to swallow was the news that Cathal's fortunes in Munster were prospering and his herds growing so large that he had had to cut down some of the neighbouring forest to make more ground for pasture.

One day, a spy employed by Fergal came bursting into the throne room and threw himself at the king's feet. He was panting for breath but the words came tumbling out: 'Your Majesty, I have such ... such news for you.'

'Well, speak, man.'

'Michael ... Michael, the Messenger ... only an hour ago he was heading out of the town when his horse stumbled on a rock in the road. Michael was thrown to the ground ... and ... and ...'

'And you come here, without so much as a by your leave, to tell me *that*,' said Fergal, getting to his feet angrily and bearing down on the spy. 'Begone, man, or I'll let you have a dozen lashes for your pains.'

'No, but please your Majesty, listen to me. All of the goods loaded on his pack spilt across the road and ... and ...'

The spy paused, gasping for breath.

'Yes? Yes! And what then?'

'Among those goods was a basket of gifts to be delivered to King Cathal. And the basket contained nuts, berries, apples and, at the bottom, a letter, a letter of love from ... from your sister Oonagh.'

There was a long silence while Fergal stared straight ahead of him.

'Let it be war between us then,' he said at last, his eyes gleaming. 'I'll assemble my army and march them down to Munster — to seize most of those cattle of his.'

And so Fergal went marching down south with his army. And when Cathal heard of this he assembled his army to do battle with the men from Ulster.

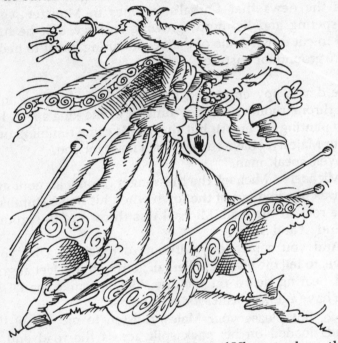

The Hag of Munster and the Hag of Ulster took up their stands on two fairy mounds by the river Barrow, near Freshford, so that they might get a good view of the battle and urge their armies into the fray. Above the wail of pipes, the throbbing of the *bodhrans* and the din of clashing swords and battle-axes came the shriek of the Hag of Ulster,

'Fergal!'

'Cathal,' shrieked the Hag of Munster.

'Fergal!'

'Cathal!'

'Fergal! FERGAL!'

'Cathal! CATHAL!'

'FER — GAL!'

'Cathal! CATHAL! CATHAL!'

'FERGAL!'

'Oh, FERGAL.'

'Ah, CATHAL.'

In the end, Fergal and his men had been driven back like leaves before a storm. It had indeed been a bloody battle.

2 ulster's king plots his revenge

ack in Ulster, some weeks later, Fergal was sitting on his throne, still smarting from his defeat, when suddenly his eyes lit up and a secret smile spread across his face.

'If I cannot gain victory by arms then I must use my wits. I'll have my way of Cathal by Art. And ... Magic!'

Turning to one of his courtiers, he barked, 'Summon Dónal of Derry!'

Dónal was a scholar and a magician, and it was said that there was no wiser man in the court when it came to the making of heathen spells. A hunched, wizened little man, he came hurrying into the king's presence and prostrated himself before the throne.

'I am told, Dónal,' said Fergal, beckoning him to rise, 'that you could, if necessary, summon up a host of demons?'

Dónal agreed that this was so.

'What kind of demons?' asked the king.

'All kinds,' said Dónal, rubbing his hands together. 'There are some who like to steal. There are some who will never let you get to sleep or, when you do sleep, give you bad dreams. And then there are greedy demons, demons of gluttony ...'

'Gluttony!' said Fergal, eagerly. 'And how big would these demons be?'

'Oh, they come in all sizes and shapes, your Majesty.'

'As small as a snail or a cherry?'

'Smaller. Tiny. So small that you can scarcely see them. No bigger than a gnat or a midge.'

Fergal reached for the basket which was destined for Cathal.

'Summon one up now. A Demon of Gluttony. Let it be no bigger than a fly. No, not bigger than a flea!'

Dónal closed his eyes, and began to mumble and make whirring motions with his hands. Then he held up the little finger of his right hand and invited the king to peer at the tip of this finger. Straining his eyes, Fergal could just make out a tiny demon with quivering horns. It seemed that this was a female imp, and Fergal thought she was actually grinning at him.

'Ask her to crawl down into this,' said Fergal, taking up an apple from the basket.

Again, Dónal made mumbling noises and invited the king to look. Sure enough, the demon had burrowed her way into the apple, for now the only sign of her was one protruding horn. A moment later this disappeared, as a worm does into the earth.

Said Fergal, 'Now I want you to take every kernel, every apple, every berry in this basket, and summon up a host of imps to make their houses in each tiny morsel.'

'Some of my imps are male and will breed with the females, once they have made their way down into the stomach of their victim,' said Dónal, in a gush of scholarly enthusiasm. 'In due time they will breed a *king* of demons who, having consumed all the other demons, will grow bigger than ever they were.'

'How big? As big as my fist?'

'Oh, even bigger. And then the victim in whose stomach

he has set up house will be perpetually hungry. No satisfying him.'

'Dónal, you can read my thoughts like a book,' said Fergal. 'Now I want you personally to deliver these tidbits of berries and kernels and apples to ...?'

The king leaned conspiratorially towards the scholar. 'Can you guess who?'

'Could it be Cathal, King of Munster?'

'Dónal, you are a wizard,' said Fergal, handing him the basket, and carefully planting the letter back just where he had found it. 'Cathal will be perpetually hungry. You shall be the richest man in my kingdom, Dónal. Now, to your work!'

3 munster's king is possessed by a demon

hree days later, Dónal arrived in Munster at the foot of the towering Rock of Cashel. He reined in his horse and hurried up the steps to deliver the basket.

It had been so long since Cathal had heard news from his beloved Oonagh that when the basket was handed to him he hastened to an ante-chamber to read in private the letter which he knew would be concealed under the sweetmeats. And this is what was written on the scroll:

'All of these scrumptious nuts and berries
and apples, laced with sugar and spices,
are for you to eat, My Beloved.
   Cathal, aroon,
   By the waves of the Sea,
   By the Sun, the Moon and the wandering stars,
   By Jupiter, Mars, and the Sisters Three
   Spinning the Loom of Destiny,
   I conjure thee –
   Munch these scrunchy apples
   For love of me.'

'Oh, I can't wait', said Cathal and took a huge bite of one of the apples.

Half an hour later, Dónal, who had mounted his steed ready to depart from the foot of the Rock, heard a great howl coming from the palace above.

'Ha! Ahah! My demons breed fast,' he said to himself gleefully, and spurred his steed northwards to deliver the news to Ulster's king.

On hearing the great howl, one of Cathal's servants had rushed into the king's chamber. He saw that the basket was empty.

'What's the matter, your Majesty?'

'I'm hungry.'

'But you ate ... you ate ... everything,' said the servant, pointing to the basket.

Suddenly Cathal held up his hand for the servant to be quiet. 'What was that?'

'I hear nothing, your Majesty.'

'A rumbling sound. Listen!'

The servant cocked his head to one side. 'I believe I do hear something, your Majesty.'

And he began to move about the chamber to track down the source of the sound, closing his eyes to help his concentration.

'What *are* you doing?' thundered Cathal, for the servant had crouched down, and his left ear was pressed against the king's stomach.

'Oh, I beg your pardon, your Majesty,' said the servant, starting back. 'But I think the sound might be coming from ... er ... your stomach.'

'Really!'

Cathal bent over to try and hear his own tummy rumbles. But, although of course he could not press his ear right up against his own stomach, the rumbles — or rather one might say the grumbles and growls — did seem to be coming from his stomach.

Suddenly he reared up, and bellowed, 'Oh, I'm so hungry. *Hungry!* I WANT SOMETHING TO EAT!'

'But you have eaten.'

'Don't keep saying that.'

'W-w-wwwwhat would your Majesty like?' asked the servant, who was now so beside himself that he had actually begun to dance up and down on the spot, like a man in the field with a hurling stick.

'A roast pig,' said the king, drooling the words.

'A *whole* roast pig?'

'Yes! A WHOLE roast pig. *And* a cow.'

Now the words came tumbling out, a veritable Litany of Food: '... Three score of cakes of pure wheat ... a vat of new ale ... thirty duck's eggs ... That'll do for a start.'

'At once, your Majesty,' said the servant, bowing and retreating towards the door, without turning his back to the king. 'I'll order your Majesty's dinner at once.'

'Dinner! Who said anything about dinner? That was just to begin with. That's my snack.'

'Oh, my God,' said the servant, panicking, and he began to shout, 'Help! Help! The king is ill! Send for the royal doctor.'

'Sssh!' said Cathal, holding up his hand again, 'That rumbling sound! There it goes again.'

And once more he bent over to eavesdrop on his own stomach. Then he reared up, and began to pant, and slaver at the mouth:

'Aaaaagh! Arrrrggh! Eruugggsssh! I'm *hungry*! I'm *so* ... hungry! I could eat:

> *Sausages sizzling from the pan,*
> *Platters of eggs, slices of ham,*
> *Legs of mutton, creamy cheese,*
> *Bacon swimming in bacon grease,*
> *Loaves and fishes, cakes and scones,*
> *Juicy melons, currant buns*
> *Noodles, bagels, honey in the comb,*
> *Rivers of treacle, strawberry jam,*
> *Nuts and raisins, kernels, dates,*
> *Heaped upon my royal plates.*
> *FOOO-OOD! I'm hungry as a wolf.*
> *Give me ... FOOD! Or I'll eat ... MYSELF.*

And Cathal took a ravenous bite at his own hand. After which he let out a howl of pain, and shook his hand up and down frantically. His roving, hungry eye now lit on his servant and was fixed there.

'Or ... YOU!' said Cathal, bearing down on the poor wretch, like a lion stalking a deer in the forest.

'Aah! Ough! Help! Help!'

So it was that the Demon of Gluttony set up house in the stomach of Cathal, King of Munster. From this time there was no satisfying his appetite, for the Demon could never have enough to eat. After eighteen months of Cathal's feastings the people of Munster came to fear that the land would be blighted with famine; Cathal was eating them out of house and home.

4 aniér mac con glín sets out for munster

ow in the Abbey at Roscommon, at about this time, there was a young scholar of great learning, a man of many gifts. He was a monk and poet, and a minstrel too; and whenever he took up his psaltery to play, it was said he could sing the savagery out of a bear. Being a poet, he knew how to mock anyone who offended him; and, in these times, the curses and withering words of a poet were greatly feared, for it was said that a poet's power with words was magical, and not of this world.

This Son of Learning was named Aniér Mac Con Glin. ('Aniér' meant that you dared not refuse him anything, while 'Mac Con Glin' meant that he was 'the Son of the Hound of the Glen'.) However those who knew him well called him Con for short.

Lately, Con had begun to feel a great yearning to leave the monastery and travel abroad. He had heard too of the feasts held in Great Munster and his mouth watered at the prospect of sitting down to one of those feasts.

One fine day he made up his mind to leave his cell and venture forth. So he sold a few things he possessed in exchange for two wheaten cakes and a slice of old bacon with a streak down its middle. These he put in his book satchel. And, on the night before his departure was due, he took a strip of hide and shaped two pointed shoes of seven-folded dun leather, to wear on the morrow.

On the next day, this Son of Learning rose early, tucked up his long shirt and wound it about his thighs, and then fastened it in a loose knot at the front. Then he wrapped himself in the folds of his white cloak and clipped it into position with an iron brooch. His book satchel he flung across his back. Then, grasping his knotty staff, he set off towards Great Cork of Munster.

It was such a grand day that Con found himself actually skipping and dancing along the road. He passed by Slieve Aughty in Connaught. Soon he was at Limerick; then by Slievefelim. Approaching the Galtee mountains, he began to feel hungry, having eaten the bacon and wheaten cakes some time earlier. He was also a little footsore, so he took off his pointed shoes and sat down by the edge of the road to rest. An old lady came out of the farmhouse by the side of the road.

'Begging your pardon, lady, this *is* the road to Cork?'

'It is right enough,' said she, wiping her hands on her apron.

'I suppose you wouldn't be able to offer a poor traveller a bite to eat?'

'Sure, I've nothing in the house but two rashers of bacon, and a jug of curdled milk from Rua the cow. She's ailing, you see, and the milk's almost gone dry on her. And then we had two bags o' the wheat, and the rats got at 'em, and sure, there's not a grain of it left now. But you're welcome to half of what I have, sir.'

'Ah no, no!' said Con, for now that he looked at the old lady at close quarters, he could see that she was lean and hollow-cheeked from lack of food.

'Rats did you say?'

'There's a plague of them in Tipperary. They made their way up from Cork when King Cathal ate his fill there.

Sure, it's only the monks who've laid in a store. There! Will you look at them now, sir!'

Con got to his feet and, sure enough, there on the edge of the field was a milling horde of rats.

'Watch out, sir! Glory be to God! Shoo! Shoo! The brazen wretches! You shoo them away and offer them a curse, and they stand up on their hind legs and grin at you.'

'Ah, but did you never try giving them a curse in rhyming verse?' asked the poet.

'No, I never heard tell of such a thing.'

'Listen! Watch!'

And Con advanced towards the seething mass, and began to intone, 'Rats! Beware of cats — Rats!'

At once, the rats became as still as graven images. Con went on, and now he was almost singing the verse:

> *Cats that hiss and cats that spit,*
> *Tabby cats, cats black as soot,*
> *Mewing cats and cats that purr,*
> *Mangy cats who've lost their fur . . .*

Now he held up his hand, as though conjuring:

> *Cats by the dozen and the score,*
> *A thousand cats, cats more and more,*
> *Brown and blue cats, cats vermilion,*
> *Cats by the hundred, thousand, million!*
>
> *Countless cats all on the prowl,*
> *Slanting, sloping, cheek by jowl.*
> *How they hiss! O hear them howl!*
> *Watch them pounce! Miaouw! Miaouw!*
> *Miaouw! Miaouw! Miaouw! Aaaah! Oooow!*

At these last sounds, the rats retreated in a mass — as though a magic carpet were moving under their feet. They scurried and tumbled over one another, they tangled in

each other's tails. A few moments later, and they were
no more than a smudge on the horizon.

The old woman scanned the distance until the last rat
had gone. Then, turning to Con she grasped his hands
gratefully. 'You're a miracle man, sir, no less. But won't
they be after coming back?'

'If ever there's rat bold enough to show his face round
here again,' said the poet, 'just you think of that poem.
No rat can stand up to that.'

'How can I ever thank you, sir? You're welcome to all
I have.'

'Ah, not at all. Just wish me well on the way to Cork.'

'Safe journey, sir!'

So Con continued on his way.

A few miles further on, he came to the country of the
Fir Feni, which is today called Fermoy. He noticed that
now, far from being a lone traveller, there were many others
who, like himself, seemed bound for Cork.

'Will you look at that now!' said the poet to himself,
'Monks pouring down into the vale of Cork like dark ale
from a barrel, and it spurting its heart out ... a dribble
of monks ... a stream of monks ... a very Blackwater of
holy monks, and all bound for the city of Finbarre himself!'

Turning to one of the monks, Con addressed him: 'Why
are they all making for Cork?'

'Sure, 'tis for the Feast of Saint Barre and Saint Nessan.'

'Feast,' said the poet, his mouth beginning to water. 'Oh,
good.'

'But that's not till Monday. Till then, 'tis a time for fasting.'

'It would be, of course,' said Con, and his heart sank,
for the pangs of hunger were now coming upon him
fiercely.

The monks had begun to chant, and the song they sang
told the story of Finbarre and how he came to found the
grand city of Cork.

Grand city it was indeed. Con and the monks threaded their way over bridges, across fords and along grassy riverside walks, to pass around the city itself. Finally they climbed the south-western slope and arrived at Finbarre's famous monastery, Gilabbey. It was perched on a craggy height overlooking the southern branch of the river Lee, and commanded a magnificent view of the town.

Con felt his heart lift up at the prospect, but was much dashed when he was turned away at the gates, while the other monks were escorted to their comfortable quarters.

'No shelter here for the likes of yourself,' said the gillie, observing that, by Cork standards, the poet's dress did not make him look like a real monk at all.

'You see, I'm a monk with a difference,' Con explained with a little smile.

'Ours is a strict order,' replied the gillie. 'We'll have none of your easy northern ways here, my lad. A monk should be dressed as a monk. 'Tis that kind of looseness that's the undoing of Our Mother Church.'

With that the gillie slammed the iron gates in Con's face. Then turning to the other visiting monks, he beckoned them to follow him.

But there was one resident monk, a fresh-faced young

man with burning eyes, who lingered at the rear. Before turning away he had smiled warmly at Con.

Con stood at the gates, gripping the bars with both hands and wedging his face between them. His heart sank. And then, when the rest of the party had disappeared into the refectory, the young man turned and, before ducking his head and disappearing through a low archway, he waved to Con. For a moment the poet felt that he was not quite alone in the world.

Con wandered through the streets of Cork. The weather had turned cold and blustery. All the shops were closed, with their shutters up, and the streets deserted. Wisps of thatch and ashes from the chimneys, mingled with flakes of sleet, blew against his cheeks. Con shivered.

Crossing over the bridges and fords that linked the islands of the city, he made his way out of Cork and stopped on a hill overlooking the Lough at Togher. There, on the south side of the hill, was a huge rock with a deep recess in it, a snug hollow which had given shelter to many a shivering wayfarer. Con huddled into it and tried to settle himself to sleep. He was about to nod off when he heard a low snarling noise and felt teeth clamped about the heel of his left foot.

'Curse you, cur,' said Con, and the dog retreated several paces:

> *Son of a bitch,*
> *Begot in a ditch*
> *By the charm of a witch.*
>
> *Winter, summer,*
> *Indoor or outdoor,*
> *By cabbage patch,*
> *Under thatch,*
> *In a ditch,*
> *Or sprawled at the foot of a larch or birch,*

May your scabby fur
Twitch and itch.
Until you scratch
And go on scratching
For evermore.

Itchy cur!

The dog slunk off down the hill, its tail between its legs. Then, stopping at the edge of the Lough, it sat back on its haunches and, lifting up its right hind leg, began to scratch and howl. And SCRATCH. And SCRATCH.

A wave of pity for the brute came over Con and he opened his eyes and sat up.

'Sure, the poor tormented creature is hungry like myself,' he thought; and, relenting, he began to whistle a sweet tune he had once heard an old woman crooning over a cradle by the shores of Lough Corrib.

Carried on the wind the tune reached the dog. Pricking up its ears it left off scratching and howling and was still for a moment. Then, having slowly turned around on itself three times, it coiled itself into a furry ball and was soon sound asleep.

5 an angel in disguise

oon Con too fell into a deep sleep. And he began to dream. About food.

At the top of the hill a soft white light appeared. And into that light walked the figure of a monk. It was the young man who had waved to Con. But now he was dressed in a long white gown.

He drew close to Con. Then, reaching into the folds of his gown, he drew forth a silver pipe. Putting it to his mouth, he began to make gentle ripples of sound, which wafted up on to the heights of Gurránabráher, and then came dipping and plummeting down again, like so many little cascades.

But if Con heard this heavenly (for so it seemed) music then he must have thought it all part of his dream, for his eyes remained steadfastly shut.

Now the monk glided behind him and spoke softly into his ear, 'You sleep soundly and you with no supper to line your belly.'

With a start, the poet opened his eyes, and became aware of his surroundings.

'Aah! Who's that?' he groaned, then shuddered. 'Awake! I was out of this world.'

The young monk now came and stood in front of him,

but Con's eyes were too bleary with sleep to see him properly.

'Why did you drag me back to this land of sorrows?' he protested, and closed his eyes tightly, as though determined to find oblivion again. 'Oh, I'm so cold,' he murmured as he tried to huddle himself into a ball.

The young monk held up his hands so that the palms were facing towards the poet. His fingers seemed to vibrate like aspen leaves in the wind and with hands thus raised, he moved slowly around the rock.

In that chilly night, Con felt such a draught as comes from the oven when the baker opens it, to reach in with his long shovel for the freshly baked bread.

Now the monk lowered his arms and once again took out his pipe.

Con shivered again. Then, as once more he heard the sound of the pipe, he opened his eyes in wonder and sat up.

'Sure, there's a sound would lift up the heart of an unfortunate man. A shepherd, is it?'

From high above Sunday's Well and the Foxes' Wood came the sound of a harp. The young monk took a few steps forward, so that the poet could see him in all his glory. To Con it seemed that there was a light wrapped about his shoulders, like a mantle.

'Is it a man of God you are and you all in white?'

But now that he was awake the pangs of hunger were on him again and he put his hands on his belly as if to comfort it.

'I've such a black hole down here in the wastelands of my belly.'

'Reach into your pocket!'

'Now what would be the use of . . .'

But when his hand dipped into the pocket, Con's fingers closed on the crusty ridges and hollows of a bread roll.

Without bothering to ask any questions, he gulped it down. Then he began to sob, and to sob again. Then he began to laugh. And to laugh again.

'Is it dreaming I am? What sort of man are you at all? Ah God, now the thirst is on me. 'Tis the salt in the bread.'

The monk gestured, as if this were the easiest thing in the world to remedy, and there, shimmering before Con, was a golden goblet of red wine, on a silver platter.

When this was duly dispatched, the poet found breath enough to speak:

'That drop of wine might have come from the groves of Italy or the Holy Land itself,' he said, wiping his mouth.

And he went tripping about on the green, and executed a little dance — finishing with a hop, a skip and a jump.

'You're an angel,' he said, overcome with gratitude. Then, as for the first time he saw the monk at close quarters, he gasped, 'Begod you *are!* An angel itself.'

And, hastily, Con made the Sign of the Cross.

The young man (or could it be a woman?) smiled. 'Now don't go letting on, but I'll not deny it to yourself.'

And, bowing gracefully, the angel said, 'The angel Mura at your service.'

'Holy God, and you a monk in the monastery, Mura!' said the poet, recognising him. Mura put a finger to his lips. Then, after looking over his shoulder, he turned back to the poet. It would not be true to say that there was a twinkle in his eye; rather there were a thousand twinkles in his eyes, for they shone like stars.

'One of God's spies.'

Having been let into such a secret, Con lowered his voice to a delighted whisper, 'But the white you're wearing! Wouldn't that give the show away?'

'I wasn't in white when you saw me before, was I?' the angel chuckled. 'This is for night wear only. By day I'm dun-coloured, along with the rest of them. I can change

shape at will when God's eye is fixed on me. Look!'

And when Con looked again he saw that the folds of the angel's cloak, which lay about the shoulders, had raised themselves up as though billowed by a light breeze.

'Wings!' breathed the poet.

And now his questions came bubbling out like water from a holy well — and it replenished by the spring rains.

'Are you a man or a girl or what are you at all?'

'A bit of both. Like all angels.'

But the poet was still overcome by the radiant beauty of the angel, who now sat down on a stone.

'The handiwork of God,' he murmured, and sat down beside Mura.

'He made us all.'

Suddenly Con shivered. 'Sure there's dew in the air now right enough.'

'Touch me!' said Mura.

Laying his hand on the downy left wing of Mura, it felt as warm and soft to Mac Con Glin as the feathers of a gosling, and it just crept out from under its mother's breast.

'You're like a fire, Mura.'

As he spoke, he heard the golden sound of the harp again and, looking up, saw a great light in the sky shining down from between a rift in the clouds.

'What's that? Up there on the hill?'

'Well it's not the dawn. Nor the moon neither.'

'Is it not? Holy God!'

The poet had broken out in such a sweat that he took out his napkin, and began to dab at his brow. Slightly embarrassed, he said to Mura, 'You'll not mind if I shift myself away a little? I'm after coming out in a holy sweat.'

Mura smiled. 'The warmth that's in me is a gift from God, but it can be too much for a mortal man to bear.'

'Well it's a blessing for all that ... Oh, excuse me.' Con's belly had rumbled so loudly that Mura looked startled.

'I'm not really hungry any more,' the poet said with an apologetic smile. 'It's just that me belly has forgotten its good manners. Sure I've a lively appetite and the belly knows it.'

He grinned ruefully. 'Sometimes the pangs in me belly set me dreaming of a land where the feasting never ceases.' He sighed. 'If only there were such a place.'

'Ah, but there is so.'

'You don't tell me.'

'The Land of Gobel O'Glug.'

'I never heard of that.'

'Where the sun goes down. Beyond the Blaskets. And further. Where the waves spill over the edge of the world.'

Con got to his feet. 'How would I be finding my way to a place like that?'

'The first thing you'd have to do would be to go to sleep.'

'Ah it'd only be a *dream* of eating then,' said Con, disappointed.

'Well ... yes ... and ... no,' said Mura, with a little smile. 'But never mind about that for the moment. Will you be going to the great feast tomorrow?'

'The Feast of Finbarre? Now you know very well I'll not be there at Gilabbey. Why, you saw them turn me away at the gates.'

'No, I'm talking about another feast. The feast in West Cork. At Drimoleague. To be given by the Lord Brian.' Did you not hear tell of that?'

'Never a word,' said Con.

'Well I'm sure you'd be welcome there. You could dance, spin yarns, sing songs for your supper.'

'And I could too.'

'Will you be going then, Con?'

'I will so,' said Con with sudden resolution.

'All right then, back to sleep now and you'll wake refreshed in the morning and all set for the road. Close your eyes, Con.'

And, when Con did so, the angel laid a soft hand on his shoulder. 'Oh and, Con,' he whispered, 'Don't forget about the Land of Gobel O'Glug.'

'Ah, you're joking me,' mumbled Con as he dropped off into a blissful sleep.

Mura moved to the top of the hill and looked down towards the sleeping poet.

'Bless you, Con. You don't know it now but you'll be seeing me again before long.'

And the angel was gone.

6 con goes
to another feast

It was the morning sun shining in his eyes which awoke Con the next morning. He yawned, stretched himself and, coming out from the hollow in the rock, looked up at the sky. Not a cloud to be seen in it. A light westerly breeze ruffled his hair.

'Well that'll be the way I'm heading,' he said to himself and, grasping his knotty staff and slinging his book satchel across his back, Con set off for Inniscarra, a distance of about a dozen miles. It was about noon by the time he arrived at that lovely little town on the banks of the river Bandon and, by this time, the pangs of hunger were beginning to come on him again.

Heading towards him, and obviously bound in the direction of Cork City, was a farmer's wife who was leading a donkey laden with milk churns and other provisions strapped on either side of its back. Noticing that the poet seemed to be scanning the side of the road she sensed that he might be looking for a signpost.

'Where are you heading, sir?' she asked.

'Why, Drimoleague.'

'Well, you cross the bridge, then follow the winding road to the right that runs all the way alongside the river to Bandon.

43

'Now, when you get to Bandon, make sure not to head south-westerly for Clonakilty whatever you do but go directly west. 'Tis a little short of forty miles from here to Drimoleague. Safe journey, sir.'

'And to you, dear lady.'

'Oh, and before you go,' said the farmer's wife. 'You look as though you could do with a drop of the buttermilk to fortify you and settle your stomach for the journey. Here now, take a sup of this,' she said, taking out a ladle and dipping it into one of the churns.

'God bless you,' said Con, having gulped down the buttermilk.

'And take this to lie atop of the buttermilk and keep it easy,' she added, handing him a buttered honey roll.

Con took the buttered roll and, bowing his thanks, assured the farmer's wife that Heaven would reward her. Then, munching on the roll, he headed blithely for the

bridge. He was scarcely half way across when a bronzed man astride a horse and leading another, halted by him.

'Are you for Bandon?' he asked the poet.

'Indeed I am.'

'You'd oblige me then if you was to get astride of this mare of mine. Then we'll cover the distance in no time.'

This certainly did seem to be Con's lucky day; for, once at Bandon, this same man sought out an acquaintance whom he knew would be taking a wagon of hay towards Clonakilty that morning.

'You'd greatly assist my friend if you'd go by Dunman-way. 'Twill add but a few miles,' said the horseman. 'And here's a tub of the goat's cheese for your pains.'

'I'll do that then,' said the farmer. ' 'Tis a bargain. But your man will have to cover the next few miles on foot for, after that, I must head south.'

So, after saying farewell to the farmer at Dunmanway, Con set off in high spirits, for the sun was still high, the sky was blue, the larks were trilling and, at each hill, the road seemed to come up to meet him, so that he hardly had to toil up it at all.

7 king cathal comes to the feast

rrived at Drimoleague, Con was extended a hundred thousand welcomes and more; and, when the Lord Brian saw the poet's tin whistle tucked into his belt, he insisted that Con entertain the company, in preparation for the feast. The poet was only too willing to oblige and, at once, took off his cloak and donned a shorter one of four pleats, as more becoming to a jester. Soon everyone was singing and dancing along with him, until they were out of breath. Then Con began to tell jokes which had them laughing and, at one point, the poet executed a little dance, which involved his coming to rest from time to time in a squatting position. Each time he went down on his haunches he broke wind, and this had the company rolling about in an uproar.

But the poet had noticed that, while this was going on, there were signs that all might not be well. A messenger had come hurrying into the Dun and whispered a few words into Brian's ear, at which the smile went from the Lord of Drimoleague's face, and he looked grim and anxious.

When the poet had done with his tricks, the rest of the company began to quaff the ale, which was being scooped out from great vats into wooden mugs and bowls. Con went across and bowed to his host.

'All very well for you and others to laugh, O Son of Learning,' said Brian. 'You'll not catch me at it. I'm after having some desperate news. King Cathal, with the hosts of Munster, has heard tell of our feast and is heading down here from Macroom; and, though they'll eat their fill, Cathal will eat ten times more than the lot of 'em. He'll gorge himself, him and that Demon that's made a house in his belly.'

'Holy Finbarre!' said Con, smacking himself on the brow. 'Why did I not think of that before?' for it dawned on him now that his attendance at this coming feast might be part of a mission set for him by the angel Mura.

'Listen,' he said to Brian, 'what would you be giving me if I were to find a way of beating down the great hunger that's in Cathal so he'd not be eating you out of house and home?'

'Well ... I'd ... I'd give you a golden ring ... and a Welsh steed into the bargain.'

And Brian held out his right hand eagerly, as though to seal the bargain.

'Holy God, is that all!?' said the poet, for such a reward hardly seemed sufficient for the task he would be setting himself. Brian was desperate enough to increase his stake at once.

'And, besides, I'll give you a white sheep levied from every house from Drimoleague to Bantry Bay.'

'Done!' said the poet. 'But do me out of my dues, and poets and satirists will scathe, scourge and denunciate you and your children's children till the trumpets sound on Doomsday.'

'You've my pledge on it,' Brian assured him.

And so they clapped hands, and it was sealed between them. Then, Con got down to business.

'Now tell some of your men to bring me your Warrior's

Stone of Strength,' said he.

Brian was aghast. 'It weighs thirty stone and more,' he protested.

'Do as I say.'

Since there was nothing else for it, Brian clapped his hands and ordered four men to come forward. When they heard this order the men began to demur but Brian was adamant.

While the men were staggering in with the massive stone Con explained to the Lord of Drimoleague that he needed it as a grindstone with which to sharpen his teeth. When Brian looked perplexed, he said, 'Oh there'll be a mighty feast all right. But ...' he added enigmatically, 'it might be a few days before we get our teeth into it.'

Once the stone was in position in a far corner, Con squatted down and, pulling his cloak over his head, pretended that he was sharpening his teeth on it. In fact he had taken a large rough file he had seen by the hearth and was dragging the file's jagged teeth across the face of the stone. So excruciating was the rasping noise that Brian held up his hands to his ears to shut it out.

The noise grew louder. And then it began to dawn on the company that an even louder noise, from outside, was overwhelming the sound of Con grinding. A messenger came rushing in and shouted something into Brian's ear, and the Lord of Drimoleague got to his feet in alarm and held up his hands for silence. Everyone realised that something momentous was afoot, and Con desisted from his grinding. A moment later, to the swirling sounds of Uilleain pipes and the beat of the *bodhrans,* the hosts of Munster came marching into the Dun; and there, in their midst, born on a litter carried by a dozen panting, sweating men was Cathal, the bloated King of Munster.

8 the king
is made to fast

elcome, great King of Munster,' said Brian, bowing so low that he seemed likely to lose his balance and topple over. Then, dipping his hand into a basket of apples, he picked out the ripest, rosiest one he could find and offered it to the king.

'Would you care for an apple, great King?'

King Cathal got to his feet, not it might be said without the assistance of three sturdy men; for Cathal was enormous. His belly jutted forth like a great promontory thrusting into the ocean. He glowered and subsided on to the floor.

'An apple?' he asked incredulously. 'I'll have a bushel of apples. A windfall of apples. I'll have a whole orchard of apples.' And, reaching into the basket, he selected the biggest one he could find, and raised it to his mouth.

Now at that very moment, Con thought fit to resume the grinding, and the noise was so hard on the ear that King Cathal shuddered, and desisted from his bite.

'What's that infernal noise?' he growled.

Brian quaked. ' 'Tis ... 'tis ... well, it's a poet, your Majesty. He's ... er ... grinding his teeth.'

49

'A poet? Hmm! And a hungry one too, I'll warrant. Set him before me.'

And Con was escorted before the king.

'So, 'twas you, was it? And who might you be?'

Con bowed:

> *King Cathal, I am Mac Con Glin,*
> *Son of the Great Hound of the Glen.*
> *For book and verse I'm yer man,*
> *Master of words, I make 'em scan.*
> *I line 'em up so they keep in time,*
> *March to the beat of a lively rhyme.*
> *I make 'em leap, caper, prance,*
> *Watch 'em skip and hop and dance,*
> *Vault and tumble, go through their hoops.*
> *Sometimes they stumble. Oops! Oops!*
> *Monk, Jester, Travelling Man,*
> *Juggler of words, catch-as-catch-can,*
> *Aniér Mac Con Glin, the poet.*
> *People call me Con for short.*

'Call yourself a scholar too, I suppose,' growled Cathal. Then leaning forward, with a menacing look, he said, 'Well, here's a thing for you to learn, Aniér Mac Con Glin. Don't grind your teeth. It puts me off my food.'

'If only it would,' said Con in a loud whisper to the court, at which a few dared to titter.

'What did you say?' thundered Cathal.

'I was sharpening my teeth because I was hungry.'

'You are hungry?' The king's eyes seemed about to pop out of his head. '*You* are hungry?'

And again the king raised the apple to his mouth. But, before his teeth could clamp down on it, Con was at his side and gently nudging him.

'What are you about now?' growled Cathal.

'I'd hate to see you eating all alone,' said Con, in a

persuasive voice. 'If travellers from far-off lands came here looking for Irish hospitality, would they not be shocked to hear of such a thing? So ... when your chin wags let it wag along with mine.'

And, with a winning smile, he sat down there and then right beside the king.

Cathal turned to look at him in amazement; for never before had he known anyone, not even a poet or a jester, who dared to speak to him in this manner and, truth to say, was even more bewildered than he was angry.

'Er ... you've not said Grace yet, you know,' said the poet discreetly. 'Never mind, I'll say it for you.'

And he clasped his hands together and closed his eyes, while Cathal felt bound to follow suit. Bowing his head, Con said, 'Bless us, O Lord, for what we are about to receive, and us ever mindful of Your Word that ... " 'Tis better to ... *give* than to receive." '

And the Son of Learning extended an open palm to the king. The court waited with bated breath. Then, after a moment, Cathal rummaged in the basket, and picking out the smallest apple he could find, he offered it to Con.

The court gasped. The hosts of Munster looked on in wonder. Never before, in all the orgies of banqueting in which they had taken part with the king, had such a thing happened. But the poet had not finished with Cathal. Far from it!

Putting by the apple with his right hand, Con said (and now his tone had altered, and he spoke in a voice which was thought becoming to a monk or other members of the clergy). 'In Learning we all know that *two* things are better than one.'

Cathal grunted and handed over a second apple.

'And a third,' demanded the poet. 'The number of the Trinity. Three's better than two.'

Cathal looked dazed. As if in a dream, he passed over

a third apple.

'*Four* books to the Gospel,' said the poet, promptly.

Cathal handed over the apple, and then, grunting and bellowing like the great brown bull of Cooley, by an extraordinary effort of will, the bloated king of Munster lumbered to his feet, and stood there puffing and panting. Clouds of steam seemed to issue from his nostrils.

Con rose. He felt his confidence beginning to ebb. Had he gone too far? Had his inspiration deserted him? His knees shook, and he began to back away, while the king bore down on him. Cathal was trembling all over and seemed endowed with superhuman strength. So great was his fury that he actually seemed to swell in size. One of his eyes had gone leaping back into its socket, while the other was as big as a heathpoult's egg. With quivering fists, Cathal raised his arms and then stamped on the ground. The earth seemed to shake, as if a great gale were abroad and the wattle and daub roof might come tumbling down and overwhelm them all.

Con gasped. And then it struck him that the strength pitted against him was not that of the King of Munster, but of Satan himself.

'Holy water for the love of God!' he whispered to one of the court. While Cathal continued to stamp and snort, this was quickly passed to the poet and he sprinkled it towards Cathal with the tips of his fingers.

But Cathal held his ground and, though his left hand had dropped to his side, his right hand was still raised aloft, like a great boulder about to topple down on a traveller in a mountain pass.

In a wild moment of inspiration, Con reached into the folds of his cloak and brought forth a small crucifix, beautifully wrought in bronze and silver. He held it up before Cathal, like a bold warrior brandishing his sword, so that it almost touched the king's fist.

Cathal stopped shaking and so, for that matter, did the walls and roof of the Dun. He froze like a statue, his eyes, no longer fierce, glazed over as though the pupils were of lapis lazuli set in the whiteness of marble; his arms and legs, which had seemed to swell to the girth of a mighty oak, now seemed no more threatening than the limbs of a sapling birch. Cathal, King of Munster, crumpled and shrank. He broke out in a fit of trembling, his teeth began to chatter, he teetered on his feet. Then, subsiding on to a stool, he buried his head in his hands and began to sob and groan.

The poet knelt by his side. But he was not touched with pity, for he knew that the battle against the Demon was far from won. So, steeling himself, Con waited for the king to speak.

'Verily, by Saint Barre, you'll devour me if you go on like this,' pleaded Cathal. Another spasm shook him, and he began to pound his stomach with his fists. 'O, I've the terrible pangs upon me,' he moaned. 'O, the great hunger. Oooogh!'

'Before you eat you must grant me a boon,' said Con quietly.

The king turned to Brian in desperation. 'Brian, did you hear that? What should I do?'

'He's a holy man,' said Brian diplomatically. 'You saw the crucifix. You couldn't be saying "no" to a man like that.'

'All right,' said the king, turning back to the poet. 'Your boon then'.

'First, you must pledge that you'll hold fast to your word.'

'There's my pledge,' said Cathal, clapping his hand impatiently into that of the poet.

'On your word as the King of Munster?'

'On my word before Brian and the men of Munster you'll have your boon. Now name it.'

'This it is,' said Con. 'That you go on fasting with me all tomorrow.'

'No! No!' The king rose and gripped Con by the folds of his short cloak. 'Please! Please, Son of Learning, not that! Let you rather take a cow from every gap in Munster.' And, desperately, he began to pile on more inducements. 'An ounce of wealth from every man who owns a house. And my own stewards will make the levy themselves.'

But the poet was not to be tempted, not even if the king were to offer him the whole of the southern half of Munster itself. Joining his hands together in a gesture of prayer, and looking up to heaven, he said, 'All I ask for here on earth is poetry, for my treasure is only in Heaven.'

The king continued to appeal to the poet, but to no avail, for Con knew that, once granted, a boon must be honoured.

When the sun began to set, Brian summoned the *ceoltóiri* (the musicians) and whispered to them that they must play the 'Sleeping' strain of music, for he knew that Cathal would never go to sleep otherwise nor, for that matter, would anyone else in the court — what with the king's moans and groans.

So, when the harp began to play its sweet unearthly music, Cathal's eyes grew heavy. After giving a great lugubrious sigh, he nodded off and was laid out on a couch.

Then all the court, with the exception of Con and the musicians, fell to slumber too.

9 con's fabulous journey

he poet took up a book to read, and now and then cast a vigilant eye towards Cathal, in case he should be aroused by the Demon within and the court taken unawares. And the *ceoltóiri*, went on playing its sweet unearthly music.

Soon all of the musicians, save the harpist, had actually sent themselves to sleep. And Con's head began to droop on to his chest in time with the tinkling cascades of sound made by the harp.

He had a vision of water: Water dripping from the branches of a hazel-tree; water in a pool with shoals of flashing salmon; water in grottos, trickling over the moss-covered stones and watercress in a holy well; water in a lough and he airborne like a swallow skimming over the face of it; ripples of water spreading out until they dispersed among the reeds and shallows of the lough; rivulets and streams of water running down into the mighty Shannon, bearing him out to a vast expanse of water — the ocean.

And now he was in a curragh in full sail. Now out on the open sea.

'Holy God, where am I at all?'

A peal of gay laughter came from above and there,
hovering over the mast of the curragh and in full flight
was ...

' 'Tis the angel Mura himself,' cried Con. 'What are you
doing?'

'I'm blowing up a wind for you, Con.'

And the angel seemed to take a deep breath and glide
behind the curragh; then, opening his mouth, he let out
a blast which sent the curragh speeding forward at an
almost alarming speed, so that Con had to grasp at the
tiller to keep the craft on course.

'You're on a journey, Con.'

'You don't have to tell me that.'

'But oh what a fabulous journey this is going to be.
'Tis a feast you're bound for, Con.'

'A feast!' protested Con, shouting over the wind.

'There was no place for me at Finbarre's feast, and Brian's
feast has yet to get under way and I'm ... I'm hungry
... and now you tell me I'm bound for *another* feast?'

'That's right, Con,' called Mura, who was now flying
alongside the curragh and leaning in to speak to the poet.

'But where will *this* feast be?' shouted Con over the noise
of the rushing wind, which now seemed to be blowing
of its own accord.

'In the Land of Gobel O'Glug of course.'

'And when I get there can I eat as much as I please?
There's food aplenty?' asked Con in a desperate voice.

'In the Land of Gobel O'Glug there's nothing *but* food.
But before the feasting there must always be a fasting.'

'Holy God, no — not *more* fasting,' pleaded Con.

'At the end of your journey you'll come to the Wizard
Doctor's Dun, where he will offer you all manner of foods.
But, on the way, no snacks, Con, not so much as a nibble
until you get there. And then, oh Con, what a feast *that*
will be.'

'No, but look here, Mura,' shouted Con, 'I don't want to cross words with an angel, but ...'

Mura had soared above him and at once disappeared into a drifting cloud.

With his hands grasped firmly on the tiller Con had a fleeting vision of the Blasket Islands and then, further to the south, the towering rock of Skellig Michael, where he had been told there was a newly founded monastery perched on the heights.

'They're close enough to Heaven,' thought Con with wonder; but soon both Skellig Michael and its companion island, Little Skellig, had faded from sight.

So the curragh sped on, and not even the falcon, the fastest of any bird that flies, could have kept pace with it. Not long after, he noticed something very strange indeed.

There, on his right, was an island surrounded by a palisade, and behind it a mighty tiger, roaring like peals of thunder, which was whirring round and round, so fast that it made the poet dizzy just to look at it. This monstrous tiger's skin was transparent and sometimes, when it came to a standstill, Con could see the tiger's body whirring round and round inside the skin. Then, for a change, the body would stand still while the skin revolved — like a weathercock in a gale, or a spinning-top.

And the poet remembered the stories of the voyages of Mael Duin and Bran, and of Saint Brendan, the Navigator, too.

'They must have seen all this surely,' he said.

Further on, he came across another island — which was inhabited by birds of such bright plumage that he had to avert his eyes. And from this island came the sound of the most bewitching music.

Then his curragh passed so close to another island that he could make out the happy faces of people gathered on the strand to wave to him. They all had cheeks with the rosy bloom of the apple on them. Their hair was fair, and their laughter like the tinkling of many little bells.

' 'Tis Tir na nÓg for sure,' said Con. 'The Land of the Ever Young. And that *cailín* — she was the only one who looked unhappy — must have been Niamh herself, and her still mourning for her beloved Oisín, and hoping that one day he'll find his way back to her.'

Soon Con noticed that the waves were beginning to change colour. No longer were they alternating blue and green but white; so that, when the gulls came swooping and mewing and scudding across the waves, they seemed to disappear from sight and merge into them. Dipping his finger into the sea, the poet lifted it up to his nose and sniffed.

'Holy God! Milk! A sea of milk!'

A strange aroma assailed his nostrils.

'Cheese,' said Con. 'I'd know that smell anywhere.'

The wind changed to the south-east, and he had to tack his sails and alter course accordingly. Now he noticed another aroma — sugar.

'The Land of Gobel O'Glug perhaps?' he said to himself and, lifting up his eyes, sighted a long strip of what looked very like sand. Then a lighthouse, a beacon and a breakwater hove into view. Con headed straight for them. As the curragh drew nearer, and he passed under the great arch that spanned the entrance into the becalmed sea of milk, enclosed by the harbour, he was startled to see that what had appeared to be slabs of rock were, in fact, gigantic blocks of sugar — held together by a mortar of cheese.

' 'Tis the Land of Gobel O'Glug for sure,' said Con; and moving the curragh into a bay that seemed to be overlaid with a kind of stucco of tallow and lard he dropped anchor, made the hawsers fast and stepped ashore.

10 the land of gobel o'glug

before striking inland for the Wizard Doctor's Dun, the poet walked along the strand to get his bearings. Then he squatted down on his haunches and gazed eastwards towards the horizon, marvelling at the sights he had seen on the first lap of his journey.

Trailing his fingers in the sand he scooped up a handful of it and let it run through them. Then, lifting up the fingers on which a few grains were stuck, he noticed that the grains seemed like tiny beads of glass, and a strange thought crossed his mind. He licked off one of the grains with the tip of his tongue.

'Sugar!' he whispered to himself. 'A sugar strand.'

Soon he came across a stream, and noticed that there was a whiff of apples in the air. He took a winding towpath that led along by this stream and came across a notice:

WARNING:
It is dangerous
to bathe in
CIDER CREEK

'Ah, that accounts for the smell of the apples,' said Con.

Now his gaze fell on a row of strange trees that marched along the brow of a hill. 'They *look* like cabbages,' he thought, and then the thought struck him, 'Perhaps that's what they *are*. Giant cabbages.'

As he left the towpath and struck out along a boreen that ran between two rows of hedges, he ran his fingers along the top of the hedge to his right and found he had smudged them with a light brown sticky substance. Once again he licked a finger.

'Caramel! Hedges made of caramel! And will you look at those giant carrots growing in the fields. They're as big as trees. Why they *are* trees. And those giant stalks of celery that are growing in a ring around a fairy knoll ... for sure they must be trees too.'

Soon he came across a lough. 'What a funny colour,' said the poet. 'As if the last rays of the setting sun were on it. Lough Derg we might call it back in Ireland.'

By the edge of this lough he spied a curious figure propped up on the bank, with a fishing-rod dangling in the lough. On one side of this figure was a mug, and on the other a fishing basket. Con stopped at a distance to watch and saw that, from time to time, this figure lifted up the mug and, after dipping it into the lough, took a draught to its mouth. Then, in a drowsy voice, it began to sing:

> *In Gobel O'Glug we're all eatin',*
> *From morn to night, nothing but feastin'.*
> *So you don't fancy bread?*
> *Then eat cake instead.*
> *Oh, we've lots of things to get our teeth in-*
> *To. Gobel O ... burp! Beg your parding!*

Having apologised for its burp, the figure broke off a piece from the rock it was sitting on and started to munch

it. Then, in between the gurgling and gobbling noises it was making, it resumed its song which was trailing away into a mumble. It seemed that this creature might be dropping off to sleep, and the poet was alarmed that it might actually topple over and drown in the lough. Creeping forward he tried to catch the words of the song:

Mmn ... *yam*yum ... mmn*yum*yam ... mmn*yum*yum
Mmn ... *yim*yam ... mmn*yom*yam ... um*tum*tum
Zsss-zsss-*zsss* ... zss-zss ... *zsssss*
Zss-zsss ... *zss-zss* ... zsss ... *zssssss*
Mmn ... *yam*yum ... mmn*yum*yam ... mmn*yum*yum
And there's lots more to eat where that comes from.
Yum! Zsss.

The poet could not restrain his amazement and spoke aloud, 'Holy God, a singing pudding!'

'Who said I was a puddin'?' said the figure, without turning towards him.

'So you can talk too,' Con replied, coming closer and peering at this strange figure.

'I'll have you know I'm no puddin'!' it said in a grumpy voice.

'Begging your pardon, sir.'

'I'm a pie. I like to dream I'm an apple pie. But I know I'm not really. I'm a bacon pie.'

The Bacon Pie yawned and, without shifting its position, turned its eyes on Con.

'Did you never see a bacon pie before?'

'Not one as well baked as yourself,' said Con politely.

'I see you've a way with the words. I'd have liked to get up to introduce myself, only I'm so tired from the fishin'.'

'Me, I'm Aniér Mac Con Glin,' said the poet, bowing and introducing himself. 'People call me Con for short.'

'They call me Slisheen — because I'm packed tight with the slisheens of bacon,' said the pie, dipping its mug into the lough, and drinking another draught.

'You seem to be very thirsty,' said Con.

'Would you say so?'

'All that water you're drinking.'

'Water? Not at all. This is wine, red wine. Glug!' And Slisheen drank yet another draught.

'There's another lough just there at the back of me,' he said, after belching. 'I've never seen it myself. I'd have to turn round, and that might give me a crick in the neck. Go on, have a sip,' he said, offering the mug to Con.

The poet was thirsty but resisted the temptation, remembering that he had already tasted sugar and caramel.

'No, I mustn't break my fast,' he said. 'Not yet.'

'Fast? What's a fast? If you're hungry, you eat. If you're thirsty, you take a drink. So what's a fast?'

Con felt that this was too difficult to explain.

'Well this other lough is of onion soup under a creamy

top. Perhaps you'd fancy that. Aaah! Ummm! Excuse me.'

Slisheen yawned and, humming the air to his song, began to nod off.

Con felt at a loss and, to make conversation, said in rather a loud voice, 'Lovely day.'

'What's that?' asked Slisheen, in a dreamy voice.

'I said it's a lovely day. Not a sign of rain.'

'Rain? What's rain?'

Slisheen opened his eyes and blinked several times. 'Am I dreaming or awake? I never saw the likes of you before.' He yawned again. 'Being awake's so confusing I find. The fish never bite when I'm awake. Which reminds me: Now that I'm awake, I've a terrible thirst on me.'

And, having dipped his mug into the lough, he hauled it up and drank again. Then he closed his eyes and began to sway and rock. 'Whoops! There's one now.'

And the Bacon Pie went through the motions of hauling in the line, landing a fish, and tucking it into his fishing basket.

'*Dream* fish. They're the best kind,' he mumbled. 'And the biggest too. They're so *big*. As big as ... *that*.' And he stretched his arms out to their full length. After which, he began to sing again:

> *Yes, fishin' is best when you're dreamin',*
> *In my dreams I catch great shoals of herring.*
> *Then I throw them all back*
> *Right into the lough,*
> *And the same goes for pike, trout and salmon.*
> *They won't drown, they're all good at swimmin'.*

And Slisheen slumped over as though about to sink into a heavy sleep.

Con nudged him, very gently, for fear that the Bacon Pie might topple over into the lough. Slisheen stirred and blissfully sang another couplet:

Dream fish never cease to amaze me.
Today they're just bitin' like crazy.

'Excuse me,' said the poet.

'Mmm? What!'

'Would you happen to know the way to the Wizard Doctor's Dun?'

'Sure I do. But I doubt if you'll make it on your own. And you can't expect me to show you. I'm too tired to get up. Besides, I'm due ...' He yawned. '... I'm due for me ... afternoon nap. But I ...'

He yawned again. '... I suggest you take the boreen past the Gravy Lough.'

'Where would that be?'

'Lift my hand and I'll show you,' said Slisheen sleepily.

Con raised Slisheen's right hand, which was streaked yellow and red, and pointed it inland.

'A little to the left,' said Slisheen.

Con steered the hand to the left.

'There!' said Slisheen impatiently.

The poet moved the hand again.

'No, not there,' he said sharply. '*There!*' and Con stopped rotating the arm, and let it drop back to the Bacon Pie's side.

'If you go there you'll meet Wheatsheaf, son of Milk in-the-Pail. He usually takes a stroll with his family round about this time. Ask him. He'll show you exactly where the Wizard Doctor lives.'

Slisheen yawned, and slumped over on to the rock, having first broken off a piece of it to nibble at. 'Nice ... talkin' to you ... safe journey ... Excuse me ... I must ... go ... back to ... sleep. I've a lot of fish to catch.'

A blissful smile spread across his crusty countenance. '*Dream* fish.'

And he began to snore.

So the poet pressed on. But so bemused was he by the various aromas and extraordinary sights (a beehive cell made of onion domes, a round tower constructed of slabs of honeycomb chocolate) that he lost his sense of direction, and finally sank down wearily on a log of parsnip to try and get his bearings.

A pudding — this time it really was a pudding — came flouncing by. It was enclosed in a pot, through which its feet protruded.

'Why, hello there,' said this pudding in a fluting voice. 'And what's the matter with you?'

'Oh, hello,' said Con, not all that surprised at this apparition for, by this time, he was becoming acclimatised. 'I've lost my way.' He gave an embarrassed laugh. 'Well I mean ... I haven't exactly lost my way. Because I never really knew what my way was.'

'You seem very confused,' said this Pudding Fairy, stepping as elegantly as she could out of her pot, and coming towards him with a winning smile. 'I can see you're a stranger, but you mustn't let that worry you. People are very friendly in the Land of Gobel O'Glug. Some of us are anyway,' she said, looking into his eyes. 'Like me, for instance.'

And the Pudding Fairy sat down beside him, and fluttered her very long eyelashes at the poet.

'You wouldn't be a poet by any chance, would you?'

'How did you guess?'

'Oh, a fortune-teller told me I was destined to meet a poet one day. I've been waiting a long time for you to come along. I recognised you at once.'

'How?'

'Oh ...' The Pudding Fairy lowered her eyes demurely. 'You have a kind of unusual ... smell.'

Feeling a little uncomfortable at her proximity, Con shifted a little towards the other end of the parsnip log.

'Have I? Really?'

There was a slight pause, and then the Pudding Fairy went on, 'Where are you making for?'

'The Wizard Doctor's Dun.'

'Oh that's a very long way away,' she said, clucking her tongue sympathetically. 'If you don't mind my asking, why would you be going there?'

So Con told her that he meant to attend the Wizard Doctor's Feast.

'Hungry, are you?' she said softly, moving a little closer to him on the parsnip log.

'Yes ... well ... you know ...' Con laughed sheepishly. 'A bit peckish.'

'There's lots to eat round here.'

'Yes, but I mustn't eat. Not just yet. I must fast,' he said resolutely. 'Until I arrive for the feast.'

The Pudding Fairy burst into peals of laughter and, rising from the parsnip log, seemed to double up — as far as her bulk made this possible.

'But that doesn't make sense. You must have heard that saying, "Water, water everywhere ...".'

'"And not a drop to drink,"' responded the poet, with a lame smile.

'So for you it's a case of "Food, food, everywhere ... and not a bite to eat."'

'She laughed again and then, in a more sympathetic tone, wiggling and vibrating her sides and coming closer to him, said, 'I mean, there are so many delicious things to eat round here.'

And she plumped herself down beside him again. 'Like me, for instance,' she said softly.

'You?' said Con, his eyes popping.

'They tell me I'm very tasty. You see ...' And the Pudding Fairy drew herself upright and vibrated for a moment ... 'I am a *pudding!*'

'Yes, I thought you might have been. But I didn't like to ask.'

'Why not take a bite?' she said huskily, nestling into his side, and fluttering her long eyelashes again.

'Of you?'

'Yes, me. Go on. Take a bite. I am very digestible.'

The poet was shocked. Trying to conceal his feelings, he got to his feet. 'Oh, but I couldn't.'

'Why not?' said the Pudding Fairy, following him relentlessly.

'It might hurt you.'

'I wouldn't mind. I'm meant to be eaten,' she said urgently. 'In fact, if I'm not eaten at regular intervals, I tend to get overweight. I *am* just a little overweight. You hadn't noticed?'

'No, you seem about the right size to me,' said Con tactfully.

'Ah, you're just saying that. Wouldn't you say I was just a little ... well ... fat?'

'Fat?' laughed Con nervously. 'You? Oh no, you're not fat. Oh, not at all. Not really *fat*.'

'You like me then, do you?' she asked in a rush.

Con swallowed hard. 'Er ... yes.'

'You really mean that?'

The poet gulped, and nodded his head.

'Prove it.'

'How?'

'Eat me. You said you were hungry.'

'No, no, please!' said Con, backing away.

'Eat me. Go on. Aren't you just a little bit tempted?'

The poet *was* hungry, and did feel just a little bit tempted.

'Wee ... ell ... wwwwhat are you made of exactly?'

'Fancy you not knowing that,' she trilled. 'And you call yourself a poet.'

And the Pudding Fairy began to sing and dance:

Now puddings come last on the menu,
For we are the pick of the feast.
Some don't clean their plate
Of gravy and meat.
But puddings never go to waste.

If you want to know what makes a pudding,
There's syrup and nuts and there's dates,
And raisins and plums.
Oh, so many scrum –
Ptious things in those humps on your plates.

In this Land of Gobel O'Glug
There's nothing so tasty to eat.
To prove that I'm right
Go on – take a bite.
For sure I'm not sour ... I'm ... sweee ... ee ... t.

Oh, eat me! Eat me!
I'm best now I'm brought to the boil,
Served piping hot,
Straight out of the pot,
They say I'm irresistible.

At this point she seized the poet by the hands and began
to whirl him about with her, in the dance.

Oh, woo me! Chew me!
Munch me until you're quite full.
Of all the comestibles
I'm irresistible,
I am the best of them all.

Yes, I am the best of them all.
I'm steaming, I'm hot,
I'm straight from the pot,
What a digestible, edible comestible,
I am the best of them all.

'Yes ... I ... am ... the best of them all,' she said, pressing herself against the poet.

This was too much for Con. He broke free and scuttled away, putting the parsnip log between them.

'No, I couldn't. I mustn't. I *couldn't*.'

For a moment the Pudding Fairy was speechless, and Con noticed that steam was rising from her.

'And I was boiling hot!' she hissed, flouncing away from him.

'Where are you going?'

'I'm going back to my pot, that's what!' she said in high indignation, and proceeded to step into her pot, drawing it up about her midriff like a bustle. 'That's the last time I ever have anything to do with a poet.'

And the Pudding Fairy whisked herself off into the wood.

Con breathed a sigh of relief. But, in all this interlude, he had forgotten to ask the Pudding Fairy to put him on the right track; so he decided that he would, anyway, go in the opposite direction to the Pudding Fairy, in case he should encounter her again.

After what seemed a very long time, he smelt gravy in the air and, coming out of the carrot wood, found himself confronted by a vast expanse of lough.

'The Gravy Lough,' he murmured. 'Oh, that smell is irresistible!' And, walking down the bank, he knelt by the lough's edge, inhaling deeply.

'Oooh! Delicious!'

He looked about him, but there was no one in sight. 'The angel Mura need never know. Oooh, I'll have to try it.'

Bending down over the lough he stretched out a hand and opened his mouth, ready to take a sip.

'BEWARE, MAC CON GLIN, LEST THE GRAVY DROWN THEE.'

Con froze. The voice seemed to echo through the wood.

'DROWN THEE . . . DROWN THEE . . . DROWN THEE.'

'Ah, 'tis the hunger has me out of me wits,' Con reassured himself. And he dipped in a finger and tasted the gravy. But the bank was so slippery with the lapping gravy that the poet missed his footing, went sliding down into the lough, and was soon in up to his knees.

'Ooops! I'm stuck in the Gravy Lough!'

To his great alarm, he began to sink deeper as if he were in quicksands, or in the middle of the Great Bog of Allen. When the gravy had reached his waist he began to yell:

'Help! Help! I'll drown in the gravy!'

Tramping out through the wood into the clearing came a troupe of six creatures, together with a horse and a dog. Like everyone else Con had met they were made of food. At the head of this family group was a man whose limbs seemed to be made of wheat stalks; while the bulk of his body was packed tight with grains of wheat. At his side was a lad who might have been his son, and who looked something of a country bumpkin. He had such a wide grin on his face that it seemed to stretch from ear to ear.

Instead of coming to the poet's aid, these two ambled down to the edge of the lough, while the rest of the family lurked in the background by the wood, and watched him flailing and splashing in the lough.

'I warned you, you fool, the gravy would drown you,' said the father.

> But I might just as well
> Bind rope around sand and gravel.

'Help!' cried Con piteously, as he felt himself sinking deeper.

'No helping some people,' said the father, turning to his son and shaking his head disparagingly.

The son laughed loudly: 'You might just as well ...'

Go digging holes without a shovel,	said the son.
Or preach God's word to the Devil,	said the father.
When you're hungry beg of a beggar,	said the son.
Aim bow and arrow at a stone pillar,	said the father.
Ask a nun to be a bell-ringer,	said the son.
Give your blessing to a sinner,	said the father.
Whisper in the ear of a man who's deaf,	said the son.
Laugh when you're aching with grief,	said the father.
Feed a new-born babe with mead,	said the son.
Or roast mutton before it has teeth,	said the father.
Try housekeeping without a woman,	said the son.
Treat mad dogs as if they're human,	said the father.
Prove that two twos make one,	said the son.
Ask a woman to hold her tongue,	said the father.
Leave a fortune to a miser,	said the son.
Expect a fool to make you wiser,	said the father.
Steer a boat without a rudder,	said the son.
Beget a child without a mother,	said the father.

Clearly father and son were enjoying this contest of words. The son was beaming happily at having kept up with his father, who patted his head indulgently. The father scratched his head, as though searching for a new phrase with which to outwit the lad.

Taking advantage of this lull in the contest, Con made another desperate appeal: 'Help! I'm sinking!'

But the father had coined another sentence which he now launched at his son with the words 'You might just as well ...' and the contest began again:

Tell water in a bucket not to slop,	said the father.
Or a flea on your nose not to hop,	said the son.
Expect a rich, old man to give,	said the father.
Or keep water in a sieve,	said the son.

'Blllllellllp!' gurgled Con. 'I'm up to my … pfff … teeth!'

At this, the father broke off the contest and gave his son a hearty slap on the back for having held his own so well in the last rally. Then, gazing thoughtfully down at the drowning poet, an idea seemed to occur to him.

'I suppose we'd better pull him free,' he said to his son.

And clasping his left hand to the bough of an overhanging parsley-tree to secure himself, he reached down with his right hand to grasp Con's right hand, while his son did likewise, clasping the bough of another tree with his right hand and grasping Con's left hand.

So Con was dragged free of the Gravy Lough and lay, gasping and blubbering and spluttering, on his back, his whole body besmeared with gravy.

'Wheee!' the father whistled to his dog, and the beast came scampering down to the poet and began to lick away at the gravy until, in no time, Con was clean of it.

Now that he had recovered, he got to his feet and took in this remarkable company for, by this time, the whole family had gathered at the bank and were gazing at him curiously.

'I'd surely have drowned without you,' said the poet gratefully.

'But who are you at all?' he asked, surveying a family which seemed to be made up of so many different assortments of food.

'I am Crumpet, son of Drisheen the Fearless from the Fairy Knoll of Eating,' said the father. 'But that's only my name on Thursdays and, since it's always Saturday in these parts, no one calls me that. Wheatsheaf, son of Milk-in-the-Pail, son of Bacon and Cabbage Roll, that's my real name and will tell you my true ancestry.'

Then, indicating his wife, who seemed to be made up entirely of leaves of watercress and was blinking and smiling sweetly at the poet, he said, 'Madam Cress, my wife ... Miss Curds and Whey, my daughter ...'

But Miss Curds and Whey hung her head bashfully and held back, trailing her foot along the ground.

'Shy she is,' said Wheatsheaf with a laugh. 'But what a cook!'

'What about me!' said his son, in a loud voice.

'Oh yes, and this big bully, who never stops grinning, is my son, Crubeen.'

'Haw! Haw!' guffawed Crubeen.

'Not a bad lad really.'

'Haw! Haw! Haw!' guffawed his son.

'But he can be a bit noisy. Pastry Puff is my wife's maid,' he said, taking the maid by the elbow and bringing her forward. Then, running his fingers through her hair, which was made up of sausage curls, he said proudly, 'She can braid my wife's sausages better than any maid I know.'

'Corn-on-the-Cob,' he said, as a figure advanced, carrying a load of carrot faggots stacked on his back and a bag in either hand. 'My bagman.'

Then, patting his horse on the back affectionately, he said, 'And this is my horse, Gammon, an excellent stallion.'

The horse neighed and pranced with pleasure.

'Yes, these are all the members of my family.'

'Woof! WOOF!' barked the dog.

'Oh, and I forgot Brisket, my faithful dog. *You'll* not be forgetting him.'

'Woof! WOOF!' barked Brisket and, rearing up on its hind legs, licked off the last slob of gravy that was sticking to Con's nose.

'Very pleased to meet you all,' said Con. 'Now would you be good enough to give me directions how I might get to the Wizard Doctor's Dun?'

Father and son had a moment's consultation. Then they started the volleying game again, at such speed that Con despaired of remembering all the directions.

Cross over a stile
Made of hard tallow.
Then on for a mile,
Till you come to a narrow
Ford of dried curds and wild boar's marrow.
— said Wheatsheaf, making a wry face.

To the left of the logs
By Suet Cottage,
Beware of the bogs.
— warned Crubeen.

Squashed onions and cabbage
And spinach and radish, a mess of old pottage.
— said Wheatsheaf, holding his nose.

Now hold your nose
Till Bean Row Bridge.
There the wild thyme blows.
— said Crubeen, taking a deep breath.

Through a gap in the hedge
You'll come to a forest of pear and partridge.
— said Wheatsheaf, his eyes lighting up.

There by the well
You'll hear buzzing bees.
That's Honeybee Chapel
— said Crubeen.

Its corbels of cherries
And sloes and wood sorrel and blue whortleberries.
— sang Wheatsheaf.

Now strike to the right
Along a boreen,
And you'll come to a sight ...
— whispered Crubeen.

... few poets have seen!
A chocolate cake castle, decked with coconut cream ...
— sang Wheatsheaf triumphantly

... aglow in the sun ...
— shouted Crubeen.

'THE WIZARD DOCTOR'S DUN,' whooped father and son in unison, after which Crubeen let out an almighty roar.

'Simple,' said Wheatsheaf, beaming and spreading his arms wide.

'But how can I remember all that?' asked Con with a worried look.

'Oh, but you don't have to remember it,' grinned Crubeen.

'What would be the use?' shrugged his father.

'But I thought ...'

'We were just having fun,' bellowed Crubeen. 'Rhyming again. Ah! Haha!'

And he pointed a finger at the poet, as though surely he must be acquainted with the rules of this game.

'How would we know the way?' asked Wheatsheaf, in an eminently reasonable tone of voice. 'We mind our own business.'

'It's not what you say, it's the way that you say it,' explained Crubeen. 'That's the first rule of good poetry.'

Con had never thought of poetry in this light and, unusually for him, could not think of a reply.

Seeing that the poet was still puzzled, Wheatsheaf went on, 'Only one rule we have: To talk in rhyme.'

'But you're not talking in rhyme now,' Con protested.

'Ah well, we need a rest from time to time,' said Wheatsheaf, hoping that this would surely settle the matter.

'It makes for a change,' said his son.

'When we're talking in rhyme the rest of the family never gets a word in,' said his father, with a gesture towards the rest of the company.

'Woof, woof,' said Brisket emphatically.

Seeing that Con was still tongue-tied, Wheatsheaf put an arm around the poet's shoulder and spoke confidentially: 'One thing I should warn you about before you go: Beware of the Tribes of Food. They're on the warpath at the moment. You couldn't be too careful.'

'They tell me they're very partial to roast poet,' said Crubeen, who had leaned in to listen. 'You are a poet, aren't you?'

'How did you know that I was a poet?'

'Ah!' said Crubeen enigmatically.

'AHAH!' corroborated his father and, gesturing to his family that the time had come to take their leave, he lifted his stalky right arm and waved; at which the rest of the family followed suit.

'Goodbye! Goodbye — eee!'

'God bye ye!'

'Good bye — eeee!'

And they were gone.

'But I still don't know which direction to take,' called out the poet desperately.

Left alone, Con decided that there was only one course left for him to take and that was simply to try his luck; so he closed his eyes and spun around several times, saying a prayer the while. When he opened his eyes he decided to strike out in the direction he was facing.

Not long after he came to a clearing in the wood, which looked suspiciously like the same spot where he had encountered the Pudding Fairy.

'Holy God, I must have been going round in a circle,' said Con.

He decided anyway that he badly needed a rest; so he took off his shoes and sat down on what looked to be a moss covered stone, which he had not noticed before. But the moment he was seated, he felt this 'stone' move under him, and leapt up. A long sigh seemed to come from the stone.

'Oh I beg your pardon,' said Con, for this 'stone' seemed to be a creature of sorts, and had unfolded what looked like two great fronds, or flaps, to reveal its eyes.

'I thought you were ... well, a kind of cushion. And, as I was feeling a bit footsore, I ...'

'Don't worry,' said the ball of moss in a sad voice. 'I'm used to being sat upon.'

Then it blinked several times. 'Are you dreaming or am I? I've never seen the likes of yourself before.'

'Well I don't belong here.'

'That makes two of us then.'

'What's your name?' asked Con.

'My name? Ah, you may well ask. You promise not to laugh?'

'Word of Honour.'

The mossy ball paused a moment, before committing itself: 'Egg Pillow.'

'Egg Pillow!' said the poet, as though tasting the words. 'You do look a bit like an egg. And a bit like a pillow too.'

'Would you say so?' said Egg Pillow. 'Well I wouldn't mind being an egg, and I'd have no objection to being a pillow; I'm used to being sat upon. But who ever heard of an *Egg Pillow*. It's ridiculous. There's no such thing.'

'Why do they call you Egg Pillow then?'

'What else would they call me? The name took their fancy and it stuck. Can I help how I look? I don't *feel* a bit like an egg pillow. I *feel* I might be something else,' it said intensely.

And, rolling out into the centre of the clearing, Egg Pillow spread its two fronds wide and began to sing:

What am I, who can tell?
Am I animal, vegetable or mineral?
I have a brain,
So I can think,
And a space in my face to eat and drink.
Do you think I'm a fink, or maybe a gink?
Oh, what am I?

Poor Egg Pillow's eyes drooped, and two tears began to trickle down its cheeks.

'What *is* a fink?' it asked. 'What does a gink look like?'

'I don't know. I've never seen one.'

'Haven't you?' said Egg Pillow. 'Well I can't be a gink then, can I? Maybe there's no such thing.'

I'm not a mussel nor a mackerel,
Nor an oyster – I'd be moister,
I'm not a chop, I'm not the shape,
And I'm not flat enough for a pancake.
I'm not gammon that once was ham,
Nor chicken that's off the bone,
I'm not a lemon, I'm not a salmon,
I'm not mutton dressed up as lamb.
I know what I'm not but – Ochóne –
I don't know what I am.

And, giving way to its emotion, Egg Pillow began to sob. Then, pulling in its fronds, it rolled over so that it looked like a mossy stone again.

Con went across to it and gently turned it over. Presently the two fronds were pulled back and, in a broken voice, Egg Pillow spoke to him again. 'Sometimes I think I might not really exist. But if I didn't I wouldn't be talking to you now, would I?'

It blinked at the poet, and then rolled over so that it was upright; that is to say, so that one end of its oval body was upright, and the other on the turf — which, Con now noticed, was composed of scattered bran and chaff.

'Come to think of it, you're a very unusual specimen yourself. How would you describe yourself exactly?'

'Me? I'm human.'

'Human! Mmn!'

A glimmer of hope lit up Egg Pillow's doleful eyes. 'Do you think I might be human too?'

'I don't really think so,' said Con, trying hard not to give offence.

'Ochóne! Ochóne!' wailed Egg Pillow.

'You live here all by yourself?' asked Con sympathetically.

'Do you call this living?' said Egg Pillow with a sudden burst of spirit. 'Anyway nobody wants to know me. I'd rather not know myself. Curled up all day long.'

And it began to roll about distractedly, flapping its fronds. Then it stopped, and was upright again.

'And I never stop thinking. That's all I'm good for. Nothing but think: Think, THINK, THINK!'

'You must eat from time to time surely?'

'*Oh* no,' said Egg Pillow emphatically. 'I've given up eating. I'm on a diet. Getting smaller and smaller every day. I used to be ten times bigger than I am now.'

Then, blinking at the poet hopefully, it said, 'Perhaps I'll get so small I won't really exist any more. Haven't you noticed how terribly thin I am?'

'I wouldn't call you thin.'

'When you're shaped like me I suppose nobody notices,' said Egg Pillow despondently.

Then a ray of hope seemed to light up its eyes. 'Maybe if someone were to gobble me up that might solve my problem.'

Then, lapsing back into gloom, it said, 'But that's not my only problem. Was I meant to eat or be eaten? — that's another thing I've never been sure of:

> *To eat or be eaten, that is the question.*
> *But mightn't I give someone indigestion?*
> *I'd like to think*
> *I'd be good to eat,*
> *But would I taste sour, or would I taste sweet?*
> *Be served in a bowl or on a plate?*
> *Oh, I'll never know.*

'I mean, it would be too late to ask, wouldn't it? After I'd been gobbled up?'

> *They might toast me, they might roast me,*
> *And keep turning me on the spit,*
> *Baste and spice me so I'd taste*
> *As delicious as you could wish.*
> *Then they'd munch me for their lunch,*
> *With a crackle and a crunch.*
> *But, lackaday, the cooks might say,*
> *As they brought me in on a tray:*
> *'Oh what a curious dish:*
> *Neither flesh nor fowl nor fish.'*
>
> *What am I, who can tell?*
> *Am I animal, vegetable or mineral?*

I know I'm me,
But who IS me?
I've a problem of identity,
Don't even know if I'm 'he' or 'she'.
Oh ... what am I?

This time, Egg Pillow broke into the most heartrending sobs; and then, after a while, rolled over and was still.

'Is it asleep?' Con wondered.

Poor Egg Pillow. The poet felt there was nothing he could do to help him (or her); then he suddenly recalled that he still had not got his bearings. So he leaned over and gently tapped Egg Pillow. The creature rolled over and slowly opened its eyes, which were now quite free of tears, and seemed fixed in a look of fierce concentration.

'What is it? I've a lot of thinking to do, you know.'

'Do you think you could tell me the way to the Wizard Doctor's Dun?'

'Just follow your nose,' said Egg Pillow and, curling up again, rolled off into the carrot wood.

11 con prepares a feast

entle Reader, pause for a moment! I, your story-teller, am faced with a problem. I am like a juggler who has two balls spinning in the air and must keep them both aloft. Likewise have I two stories spinning in my head. You would like me to go on with the story of Con's fabulous journey to the Wizard Doctor's Dun? Well, I'd like to oblige you BUT ...

At this moment my ears seem to be assailed by the dreadful howls and moans coming from Cathal, King of Munster, as he tosses and turns and writhes in his sleep. *What has happened?*

Ah, I see now, I see what it is. The first rays of the dawn are spilling through the door of the Dun and lighting on Cathal's eyelids and — what is more — no longer are the king and the demon lulled into stillness by the 'Sleeping' strain of music.

The harpist has fallen asleep!

Con has awoken! He sees what has happened and rushes across to the harpist and shakes him awake.

'For God's sake you must go on playing,' he whispers urgently to the harpist. 'And move your harp right alongside the king *so that he will hear nothing but your music.*'

So now the bleary-eyed harpist has begun to play again and, thanks be to God, except for the rippling sound of the harp strings, stillness reigns again in the court of the Lord Brian.

As for Con's journey to the Wizard Doctor's Dun, well this much I will say: He did, of course, arrive there and ... no, I will say no more for, in a moment, I will allow the poet to tell you about the rest of his journey in his own words ...

So, while the harp played, Con crept over to the couch where Brian lay and shook him gently. But Brian was already awake.

'Get up,' said the poet in a low whisper. 'I've a few tasks in hand for you. And no questions to be asked!'

Then he explained that preparations must be made for the feast. He wanted juicy old bacon, and tender corned beef, and full-fleshed wether, and honey in the comb; and a polished dish of English salt and, most importantly of all, a great bronze cauldron.

And, as well as this, Brian was to arouse four of the greatest warriors of Munster, who were to be given ropes and hooks and staples with which to bind and tether the king to the posts which supported the walls and roof of the Dun. Such a glowing, inspired light was there in the poet's eyes that none dared to disobey him. So all this was done to the King of Munster, as he lay on his couch, snoring and snorting.

Then Con donned a chef's cap and apron and, with the assistance of the resident cooks, began to prepare the feast. The ingredients he had ordered from Brian were procured for him, and these were speared on four perfectly straight spits carved from the boughs of a hazel-tree, and suspended over the fire which the poet himself had laid. The fire was constructed from ash wood, with four ridges and four apertures, so that it burnt without smoke and gave off no sparks. So deftly did the poet turn the spits, and attend to the various joints, that it was remarked that he was like a hind looking after her first fawn, or a roe, or a swallow, or a bare wind in late March. He rubbed the honey and the salt into one piece after another; and so careful was he in attending to the four great joints that not so much fat dropped out of them as would quench the flame of a candle but, instead, seeped down into the centre of the joints so as to make them the more tasty.

When these joints were cooked the poet took the four spits and, bearing them aloft on his shoulders, went across to the Dun where the King of Munster still lay sleeping. A delicious aroma filled the Dun, and the poet ordered the harpist to stop playing.

Cathal awoke and when this aroma assailed his nostrils, he bellowed, 'I want something to EAT!' and made to rear up from his couch.

'What's this? What's going on?' he said furiously, when he found he was bound hand and foot. 'Brian! Do you hear me?'

'It's not my doing. I swear it,' stammered Brian. ''Tis for your own good, according to the poet. Oh God, this will be the death of me,' he whispered to one of his courtiers.

Having stuck the four spits into the floor of the Dun, at the foot of Cathal's bed, Con had taken a carving knife from a rack, and was busy cutting a slice from one of the joints.

'Mac Con Glin! What are you doing?' thundered the king.

'Carving the joint,' replied the poet, with the sweetest of smiles.

'Oh yes! yes! Give me something to *EAT*,' said the king.

'Oh, but you must be patient when you come to eat, great King of Munster. Otherwise, what with your long fasting, you might choke yourself to death. Now ...'

And spearing a slice on a two-pronged fork, he moved towards Cathal, whose mouth was wide open. Then, when he was within two feet of the king, he stopped.

'I must try a slice for myself first. The champion's portion!' said Con. And he did so, having first dipped it in honey and English salt.

'Mm! Delicious!'

Then the poet proceeded to carve several more slices and, putting them on a silver platter, offered them to three of the hosts of Munster.

'Ah,' said the king. 'Aaagh!'

'The opinion of three is better than one,' said Con. 'Is it underdone?'

The three lords, whose mouths were stuffed so full that they could not speak, shook their heads.

'Done to a turn?' inquired the poet.

'Mmm! Mmmn!' they each nodded emphatically.

'Brian,' said the Son of Learning, 'You'll have to give *your* opinion of my cooking.'

And he cut another slice and, once again, slowly passed it in front of Cathal's mouth, this time holding it there for a moment so that, for Cathal, the aroma was overpowering.

'Ooogh! Aaagh!'

But, once again, Con bypassed the king of Munster and gave the meat to Brian, who gobbled it down greedily.

'Eeh!' squealed the king for, in his eagerness to bite the meat, he had bitten his own tongue. 'Eeeh!'

'Carve the food for us, O Son of Learning,' said the king in a wheedling voice.

'All in God's good time,' said Con taking another slice for himself.

'By God's doom how much longer, O Son of Learning? I'm starving!'

'You've consumed such a quantity and variety of agreeable morsels in your lifetime,' said Con in between munches, 'that ...' (gulp!) '... that it will be doing you no harm ...' (gulp!) '... to hold off a while yet.'

'Fire and brimstone!' shouted the king, straining at the ropes. 'May twenty-one demons tear you asunder! May your limbs go into the grave without a shroud! May rain and fire, ill winds and snow follow you into the grave! And, when you get there, may the snails devour your corpse ... Brian!'

But the cowardly Brian was not to be seen. He had withdrawn discreetly to the back of the assembly.

'Keep calm! Keep calm!' said Con. 'Where are the *ceoltóiri*? Ah, there you are! Now, my dear friends,' he went on urgently, 'I must call on you again. This time you must play the "Soothing" strain. For I've a story to tell.'

'A story!' said Cathal frantically. 'My God! He wants to tell me a story!!'

'About food.'

'Food, did you say,' panted the king. 'FOOD!?' he yelled. Then, as the music began to have its effect, his voice became plaintive, like that of a small child, 'Fooood?'

'Lie back now and listen,' said Con. 'You see I had a dream. Well, not exactly a dream, call it a vision. No, not a vision. I had a ... journey. To the Land of Gobel O'Glug.'

And the poet began to tell of his fabulous journey, of how he had arrived at the country where everything was made of food; of how he had met with Slisheen and the Pudding Fairy, and Wheatsheaf and his family, and poor Egg Pillow. And the king listened, enthralled.

And then Con came to tell of how, after leaving Egg Pillow, he had approached the Wizard Doctor's Dun....

12 con meets the wizard doctor

And so I advanced. Resolutely! Boldly! Fiercely! Having crossed a causeway of pastry I forded a stream of frothy lemonade. Once, in a thick mist, I found myself in a churchyard, and stumbled and fell, and struck the back of my head on a tombstone of hard biscuit. As I drew closer to my destination, I lifted my shirt up over my bum; and neither fly, nor gadfly, nor gnat could cling to that bum, so speedily did I make my way through plains and woods and wastes, towards the Magic Dun.

When the Dun came in sight, I advanced stealthily, like a fox approaching a shepherd, or a crow hovering over a carcass, or a young buck coming to crop a field. On reaching the wall of the Dun, I seized a cudgel of bone and dealt such a blow to the cheese door that it splintered the bolt that held it fast. From there I made my way to the inner chief residence of the enormous Dun. A mattress of raspberry jelly lay just inside the threshold, and on this I threw myself down, to recover my breath. And it took eight strong men to pull me out by the crown of my head.

Finally, I met the Wizard Doctor himself. To a great fanfare of trumpets, he came sweeping into the Dun. When he saw me at the other end he spoke; and everything he uttered echoed throughout the Dun, so that I heard every word.

'My friends,' said he. 'A formidable figure is amongst us. Aniér Mac Con Glin — of the men of Munster. A young feller of deep learning. Entertaining! Delightful! He must be well served, for he is a man of many moods, voracious and fond of early eating. And yet he is mild and gentle. Welcome Mac Con Glin, Son of the Hound of the Glen,' he said, coming to meet me. But, suddenly, when he came close to me, a look of great concern came across his face and, taking my hands between his own, he said:

'In the name of cheese what ails thee? Thine is not the look of a full suckled milk-calf.'

Then, turning to address the court, he gave this diagnosis: 'The three hags have attacked him — Scarcity, Famine and Death. Thy hands are yellow, thy lips speckled, thine eyes grey.'

Feeling over my body with his long fingers, he said, in a wise, grave voice, 'Thy body is like a skeleton.'

After this, the Wizard Doctor asked me to give him the symptoms of my great hunger. And so I told him that I was always hungry. That, all day long, I dreamt of food; of nutty cakes and fruit cakes and cakes of all kinds; and that, even after I had eaten, I was as hungry as ever, if not more so. I told him that my wish would be that every dish that was ever baked, fried or grilled, roasted or toasted since time began, be spread before me. And yet that, if they were, I knew my belly would still croak with the pangs of hunger; and so that was why I had come to his Dun. To enjoy a feast to end all feasts.

'Mmm,' said the Wizard Doctor, shaking his head. 'Thy disease is indeed a grievous one.'

At that he clapped his hands, and spoke to the court:

> *Poor Mac Con Glin is looking thin,*
> *He's skin and bone from toe to chin.*
> *How fortunate our meeting.*
> *Since he's an Irishman, you see,*
> *We owe him hospitality:*
> *A gastronomic greeting.*
>
> *The poor man's slavering at the mouth,*
> *For sure he's thirsty, slake his drouth.*
> *His looks bespeak a famine.*
> *His eyes wax dim, his complexion's wan,*
> *He's that far gone, he's not human.*
> *Let's fill him up or he'll become*
> *A walking, talking skeleton.*

'Summon the chefs,' he commanded.

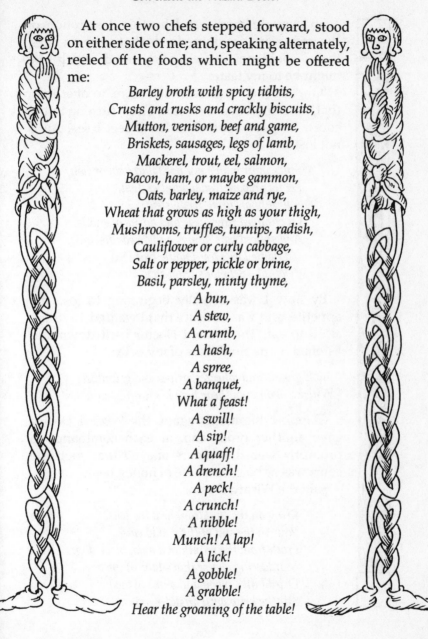

At once two chefs stepped forward, stood
on either side of me; and, speaking alternately,
reeled off the foods which might be offered
me:

Barley broth with spicy tidbits,
Crusts and rusks and crackly biscuits,
Mutton, venison, beef and game,
Briskets, sausages, legs of lamb,
Mackerel, trout, eel, salmon,
Bacon, ham, or maybe gammon,
Oats, barley, maize and rye,
Wheat that grows as high as your thigh,
Mushrooms, truffles, turnips, radish,
Cauliflower or curly cabbage,
Salt or pepper, pickle or brine,
Basil, parsley, minty thyme,
A bun,
A stew,
A crumb,
A hash,
A spree,
A banquet,
What a feast!
A swill!
A sip!
A quaff!
A drench!
A peck!
A crunch!
A nibble!
Munch! A lap!
A lick!
A gobble!
A grabble!
Hear the groaning of the table!

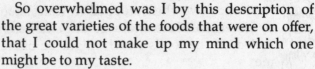

So overwhelmed was I by this description of the great varieties of the foods that were on offer, that I could not make up my mind which one might be to my taste.

'Oh, but there's more, much more, to offer than that,' said the Wizard Doctor. Then, turning to the court, he gave another order: 'I see! I see! All is not lost.'

> Since your man's not partial to fowl or fish,
> Let us prepare him a daintier dish,
> A highly original 'Irish' stew,,
> Of chopped frogs' legs and horns of snails,
> And spliced bats' wings and diced rats' tails.
>> Diddle Dee Dee! Diddle Dee Doo,
>> What a delicious Irish stew.

By now I was actually beginning to lose my appetite, and was not sure that I wanted anything at all to eat. The Wizard Doctor bent down and listened to the rumblings of my belly:

> Such groans and wheezes, gripes and grumbles!
> Whisht! Don't you hear how his tummy rumbles!

Clapping his hands again, the Wizard Doctor gave another order and, at each command, so promptly were his orders obeyed that soon the court was as busy as a hive of honey bees.

Said the Wizard Doctor:

> Bring on the cauldron, heat the vats.
> Pour in the spit of three wild cats,
> Froth from the mouth of a mad, black dog,
> Mouldering cheese that's lain in the bog.
> Dried bull's blood and slime of toad.
> Stir the brew with an alder rod.

And a chef, in black hat and gown, dipped in the rod and began to stir the brew, while the Wizard Doctor commanded more and yet more ingredients!

Leaves that were plucked from the dismal yew
One chill midnight, when the moon was blue.
Sprigs from the nest of a carrion crow
That caws in the ash-tree. Now, to follow,
Sweat of a sow that ate her farrow.
Season the brew with wild boar's marrow,
And other ingredients just as nice
From other beasties: Weasels, mice,
Fleas and flies, and bees and lice,
Wasps and gnats and owlets' wings,
Snout of a stoat, and blind worms' stings.

This was more than I could bear, and I felt my gorge starting to heave. Seeing this, the Wizard Doctor held up his hand, and the chef in black ceased to stir the cauldron.

The Wizard Doctor stroked his beard (which looked to me as it were made up of curds and whey) and pondered deeply. At last he spoke in a hollow voice:

Poor Mac Con Glin's not feeling well,
What ever can ail the feller at all?

Then, with a wild shout, he proclaimed:

I see what it is: The stew's not for you,
It must be you that's meant for the stew.
Tear him to pieces, limb from limb.
Into the cauldron with Mac Con Glin!

And, licking their lips, the whole court began to close in on me:

Tear him to pieces, limb from limb.
Into the cauldron with Mac Con Glin!
Diddle Dee Dee! Diddle Dee Doo,
What a very Irish Irish stew

they chanted, stamping their feet. With one gesture, the Wizard Doctor halted them.

'No, wait!' he said 'There must be many ways of cooking an Irish poet. Let's not be too hasty about this. What's your opinion?' he asked, consulting the chefs. So the chefs huddled together:

Shall we spit him, shall we boil him?
Shall we fry him, shall we broil him?
Shall we mince him, shall we dice him?
Shall we roast him, shall we spice him?
Simmer him, grill him, poach him, bake him?
Steam him, griddle him, masticate him?
Peel him, skin him, bone him, scrape him?
Chew and munch and scrunch and ... EAT ... him!
Every morsel, big and small,
Boils and bunions, warts and all!

The mention of all these foods, and now, of the various modes of cooking, had held the King of Munster spellbound, and deep gurgitating sounds came from within his throat and stomach. Undeterred, Con went on with his story:

Once again, the Wizard Doctor held up his hand, and the court fell silent. Then I was astonished to see a broad, generous smile spread across his face.

'We didn't mean it,' he said. 'That was just part of the initiation ceremony. And you have passed the test. There now, doesn't that make you feel better?'

So overwhelmed with relief was I by this unexpected turn of events, that I had indeed begun to feel better.

'You have nothing further to fear,' the Wizard Doctor assured me warmly. 'Now! Here is a recipe no-one can resist.'

And once more he gave orders: 'First, let a nimble, joyous woman, with hands as white as the lily, wait upon him. She must be of good repute, red-lipped and womanly, eloquent and of good kin. She must wear a necklace. And a cloak — with a brooch. And the cloak must have a black hem between its two peaks, so that sorrow may not come upon her. And the three dimples of delight must show on her cheeks ...'

'Food! FOOD! Tell me more about FOOD!' spluttered Cathal.

But Con continued. 'Patience! Patience,' he said to the king. 'The Wizard had more to say.'

'This maiden shall give thee thrice nine morsels which I shall mix, each morsel to be as big as a heathfowl's egg, and to be put in the mouth with a swinging jerk, making sure to whirl your eyes around in your head while you eat. And each to contain the eight kinds of grain; with eight condiments and sauces, mixed in a smooth pannikin of cheese curds, with a drop of the bubble-burster, new ale ...'

13 the demon of gluttony comes out

lug! Gob ... Gob ... lll ... O ... Glug!' gargled the king, with his mouth wide open. He threw back his head and now a different kind of noise came from his stomach. It sounded like the growl of a dog: 'Arrgh! Urrgh! Aaarrgh!'

Con looked down the king's throat; then, turning quickly to Brian, he said, 'My God, he's coming up! The Demon's coming up! He can't stand it any longer! I must go on with my story.' And so he resumed ...

The Wizard Doctor then said: 'Now! A slisheen of the cure of chest disease — old bacon. And the tender flesh of hazel kernels. On top of these you must drink a yellow, bubbling milk, the swallowing of which needs chewing. And it must be milk that makes the snoring bleat of a ram as it rushes down the gorge, so that the first draught says to the last draught, "I vow before the Lord there's no room in this stomach for the pair of us. And if you come down ... I'll go ... UP."'

'Urrrk! Urrrrk!' gargled the king.

'Up! Up! OUT!' cried Con, peering down Cathal's throat.

'I want something TO EAT,' howled the king.

'I ... want ... something ... to ... EAT,' came a dreadful echo from within Cathal's belly; and this time the voice was unmistakably that of the Demon itself.

Con blessed himself hastily, and said to Brian, 'Pass me a cut of the roast pig. And dip it in honey.'

Snatching up a fork, with a slice of roast pig impaled on it, Brian dipped it into the honey, and passed it to the poet.

Con held it up in front of the king's mouth, and a black, shiny, dog-like creature came darting forth, like an enormous tongue. The Demon snapped its jaws at the delectable morsel, but the poet snatched it away from its reach; and the Demon leapt out of the mouth of the great King of Munster.

The poet danced, skipped and twisted and turned about the floor of the Dun, teasing and tantalising the monster, who was snarling and clacking its jaws, and growling in such a terrifying way that the whole court had retreated to the outer walls.

So the dance went on, with Con always evading the Demon. Finally it stopped in the centre of the Dun and crouched there, snarling, spitting and hissing.

'The cauldron!' whispered Con to Brian, who was at his elbow. 'Here, take this!' And, handing the fork to Brian, he raised the bronze cauldron, upended it, and then deftly popped it over the head of the infernal monster.

'Got him!' said Con, and a great sigh of relief arose from the court.

'To God and the holy woman of the Curragh, Saint Brigid, we give thanks,' proclaimed the poet.

Then Con ordered the Dun to be cleared, for he knew that there was only one way to exorcise the Demon once and for all, and that was to burn down the Dun until

it was reduced to ashes. Tapers and torches were fetched, and soon the Dun of Drimoleague was transformed into a tower of crackling flames. At the summit of this pyre appeared the Demon, snarling and hissing, and flapping its black wings. The Son of Learning held up a crucifix, and the Demon cowered back in dismay.

'Do obeisance to us! In the name of the sweet Christ!' intoned Con.

'Indeed I will,' cried the Demon abjectly. 'For thou art a man with the grace of the seven fold Spirit. Three half years have I resided in the belly of King Cathal — to the ruin of Munster. Had I continued three half years more, I should have been the ruination of all Ireland ...'

And then suddenly the Demon changed its tone and seemed to seethe with fury. 'It is into thine own throat I would have leapt, and set up house in thine own belly. With dog straps, scourges and horsewhips through all

Ireland thou wouldst have been lashed. And the disease that would have robbed thee of thy life would have been ... Hunger. HUNGER! THE GREAT HUNGER!'

'Enough!' interrupted Con, holding up a silver case, engraved with a crucifix and containing the Gospels of the Four Evangelists:

'Look on the Gospels and behold the sign of the Lord's Cross between me and thee.'

The Demon of Gluttony cringed: 'By The Great King of Darkness, O Cathal of Munster, were it not for Saint Brigid, the fair woman of the Curragh, I would bear thy body into earth, and thy soul into Hell, before this night were out!'

But Con was indomitable, and advanced at a steady pace towards the Demon, brandishing the Gospels until, with a clatter of wings, the Demon ascended into the sky and flew towards the horizon. Then, suddenly, it plummeted down and was lost from sight.

'Where is he now I wonder?' asked Brian in a fearful voice.

'In Hell. Where else?' replied the poet with a smile. 'Where he belongs.'

14 peace between ulster and munster

ing Cathal lay stretched out on a couch, and now everyone could recognise him for the familiar King of Munster they had known before the Demon of Gluttony had possessed him and distended his belly. The Son of Learning gave orders that fresh milk, with droppings of honey, should be boiled and administered to Cathal, while this time the *ceoiltoiri* would play the 'Healing' strain.

When the king awoke he called for the poet.

'Aniér! *Aniér* indeed, for you are a man not to be denied. How can I ever thank you?' he said, stretching out his hands. Then a look of sadness passed, like a shadow, over his face.

'O I should be happy now, and yet I am not.'

'Perhaps there is someone close to your heart who is absent?' inquired the poet gently.

'Yes. Yes! O how I wish she were here,' sighed Cathal, for his thoughts had turned to the lovely Princess Oonagh. 'Then my cup would be full.'

'If only the angel Mura were here,' thought Con.

His wish was father to the deed for, at that very moment, Mura came sweeping on to the scene. At his side were

Fergal, King of Ulster ... and his sister Oonagh.

'Yes, there are times when it is necessary for me to intervene,' he smiled. Then, speaking in a firm, ceremonious voice, the angel Mura ordered King Fergal and the Princess Oonagh to step forward. King Cathal arose, full of wonder.

'I charge you two kings that, henceforward, Ulster and the rest of Ireland be at one. And in eternal Peace. And, in token of this peace between the men of Ireland and Ulster, I here proclaim the banns of King Cathal of Munster and the Princess Oonagh of Ulster.'

And, taking the Princess's hand, he laid it in the hand of Cathal:'Their wedding shall be celebrated in Great Cork of Munster ten days hence. And, for two days beforehand, the bells of Cork will ring without cease. And, from this day out, our noble friend, Aniér Mac Con Glin, the Son of the Hound of the Glen — a man who is not to be denied, for he is a scholar, a monk, a poet and a man of surpassing wit — shall sit at the right hand of the King of Munster, and lead him in the paths of God ...'

AMEN.

et this story be heard by every ear, as elders and old men and historians have declared, as it is read and written in the Book of Cork, as Mac Con Glin uttered a great part of it to Cathal Mac Finguine, and to the men of Munster besides.

There are thirty chief virtues attending this tale. Here are a few of them:

The married couple to whom it is related the first night shall not separate without an heir; they shall not be in dearth of food or raiment.

The new house in which it is the first tale told, no corpse shall be taken out of it. It shall not want food or raiment. Fire does not burn it.

The king, to whom it is recited before battle or conflict, shall be victorious.

On the occasion of bringing out ale, or feasting a prince, or of taking an inheritance or patrimony, this tale should be told.

The reward for the recital of this story is a white-spotted, red-eared cow, a shirt of new linen, a woollen cloak with its brooch. These to be offered by a king, a queen, by married couples, by stewards, by princes, to those who tell the story.